**Eduard Hanslick
and
Ritter Berlioz in Prague**

Frontispiece. Roßmarkt, now Wenceslas Square

View from the Roßtorbastei, now the site of the National Museum, towards the Old Town, with Hradschin on the far side of the Moldau in the background. The Hanslick family lived in one of the houses to our left at the lower end of the square.

GEOFFREY PAYZANT

Eduard Hanslick
and
Ritter Berlioz in Prague

A DOCUMENTARY NARRATIVE

University of Calgary Press

First published 1991

The University of Calgary Press
2500 University Drive NW
Calgary, Alberta
Canada T2N 1N4

Canadian Cataloguing in Publication Data

Payzant, Geoffrey, 1926–
    Eduard Hanslick and Ritter Berlioz in Prague

    Includes bibliographical references and index.
    Includes text and translation of Hanslick's
Ritter Berlioz in Prag.
    ISBN 0-919813-81-X

    1. Hanslick, Eduard, 1825–1904. 2. Berlioz,
Hector, 1803–1869—Criticism and interpretation.
3. Hanslick, Eduard, 1825–1904. Ritter Berlioz
in Prag. I. Hanslick, Eduard, 1825–1904. Ritter
Berlioz in Prag. II. Title.
ML423.H25P39 1991   780'.92   C91-091255-6

Cover design, incorporating a detail of a view of Old Town from Kleinseite (reproduced as Fig. 9, p. 35), by Windsor Viney

♾ Printed on acid-free paper
Printed and bound in Canada

To Jacques Barzun

Monsieur Hanslick, the bearer of this note, is a delightful young man full of enthusiasm for the great things in music. He has written about our art as one writes who has soul, heart, and understanding. I am sure you will be happy to make his acquaintance.

– Hector Berlioz, letter to Franz Liszt
dated Prague, March 26th, 1846

Contents

Illustrations

Preface

O ANYONE FAMILIAR with the careers of Eduard Hanslick and Hector Berlioz, the conjunction of their names in the title of a book may seem improbable. It is well known that the kind of music Berlioz wrote was anathema to Hanslick, who was the most influential music critic of his time. For a few weeks in 1846, however, in Hanslick's home town of Prague, the famous composer at the height of his powers was in amicable, almost daily contact with the young critic at the threshold of his career. Hanslick was then extravagantly enthusiastic about Berlioz's music, but a year later he expressed doubt in print over whether it could properly be regarded as music at all. To explain this *volte-face* is one of the tasks I have set myself in the present work.

By his own account, Berlioz experienced in Prague the most gratifying public acclaim of his career. As several local journalists pointed out, there had been no such enthusiasm in Prague for a musician since 1787, the year Mozart conducted the première performance of *Don Giovanni* before an enraptured audience there.

The encounter in Prague between Eduard Hanslick and Hector Berlioz in the early weeks of 1846 was fateful for both; yet Berlioz's visit to that city has received scant attention in the literature, his personal association with Hanslick virtually none. For this reason, and in the hope of achieving an immediacy not otherwise possible, I have gone to the sources and told the story of Hanslick and Berlioz mainly in the words of the participants themselves. The three central characters—Hanslick, Berlioz, and August Wilhelm Ambros—were among the liveliest and most renowned musical journalists of their century, so I make no apology for quoting at length from their writings. But there are a few minor characters in the story whose writings are of no less interest, so I have included generous samplings from them. Apart from Berlioz's own letters and autobiographical writings, most of my source documents were originally published in German, but few of them have been reprinted or translated. My task has been to select, translate and arrange this material, and keep the story moving with descriptions of persons, places and events, and with explanatory remarks, not to mention a few personal opinions.

As its title indicates, this book's focus is the intersection of the careers of two men at a time and a place. In 1846 the official music of Prague was for the most part German, as it had been since the seventeenth century when the Kingdom of Bohemia became an Austrian province under the Habsburgs, but in that year a resurgence of Bohemian music was in progress. Some of the most important leaders in this nationalistic movement were also prominent in the official music: the names of Kittl, Tomaschek, the brothers Škroup and the music publisher Hoffmann come readily to mind. They all appear in my narrative.

A comprehensive history of Berlioz's visit to Prague would have to take this resurgence into account and would draw upon the Czech journals as well as upon the German ones. Such a history is overdue; it would reveal, among other things, that the Czech journals were less enthusiastic about the music of Berlioz than were their German counterparts. The events I describe here took place in a primarily German context, however, and their most significant consequences were for German musical aesthetics and musical criticism. It is to these consequences that I point in my concluding chapter.

All translations are mine unless otherwise indicated. In the matter of rendering Czech and German proper names a certain amount of inconsistency is unavoidable. For example, "Pulverturm" is trivialized by the assonance and metre of the customary "Powder Tower," with its whiff of an advertisement for cosmetics, so I use the German. Likewise, "Sophieninsel" is absurd as usually translated, "Sophie's Island," suggesting (as it indeed it did to Berlioz) someone's washerwoman, not an archduchess and mother of an emperor-to-be.[1] "Schützeninsel" was translated by Berlioz in his *Mémoires* as "l'île des Chasseurs"; for much of its length this tiny island is scarcely wider than a hunting horse's leap.

---

[1] See pp. 30 and 36 below.

"Schützen" in the relevant sense are not "hunters" but "shooters," marksmen scoring hits on wooden targets with firearms, not killing wild game. The expression "Estates Theatre" does not convey much in English because "estates" have never figured in the political structures of English-speaking countries; under the name "Ständetheater" the building (now Tylovo divadlo) occupies a distinguished position in the musical and theatrical history of Europe, and by that name it was most frequently designated in the German journals of Prague in the 1840s. "Karlsbrücke" loses much in translation to "Charles's Bridge." On the other hand, by referring to the hotels as "Blue Star" and "Three Lindens" I avoid problems with the German "zum." I translate place names into English wherever doing so permits a more comfortable sentence than would be possible with the Czech or German originals, and where this procedure does not result in a loss of period atmosphere. Hence "New Town" and "Old Town," but "Hradschin" and "Kleinseite." In some instances, I also provide the modern Czech names to help identify buildings or sites. For the most part, I give personal names in the versions most commonly encountered in the German journals of the time.

The germ of this study is Jacques Barzun's brief account in his *Berlioz and the Romantic Century* (1950) of Berlioz's visit to Prague in 1846. Eduard Hanslick makes a fleeting appearance therein, as does August Wilhelm Ambros. My researches have been concerned more with these two than with Berlioz, but my enthusiasm for the latter's music dates from my first reading of Barzun's book in the early 1950s, as does my curiosity about the improbable link between Hanslick and Berlioz; hence the dedication here. Jacques Barzun commented on an early draft of this work, and provided helpful advice, but he is in no way to blame for its imperfections, nor are the many other people who provided assistance of one kind or another. I thank them all, including Steven Burns, Gordon Epperson, Clemens Höslinger, Ivo Jirásek, Vendula Jirásek, Peter Kivy, Jitka Ludvová, Mary MacKay, Keith MacMillan, Robert McRae, Jaroslav Mráček, Philipp Otto Naegele, Michael Nagy, Miroslav Nový, Paul Rauchbauer, Thérèse Salviat, Ewald Schaefer,

Windsor Viney, Alan Walker and Helga Wischnewsky.

I also thank the Humanities and Social Sciences Committee of the Research Board of the University of Toronto for a grant in support of my research in Vienna and Prague in 1987.

This book has been published with the help of a grant from the Canadian Federation for the Humanities, using funds provided by the Social Sciences and Humanities Research Council of Canada.

I

Preparations

ECTOR BERLIOZ MADE two major tours in Germany to promote his compositions and to seek recognition as a conductor. The first tour was in 1842–43, the second in 1845–46. It was on the latter that he visited Vienna and Prague; he arrived in Vienna on 9 November 1845. In his *Mémoires* Berlioz wrote:

> I had already travelled all over Germany before it occurred to me visit Bohemia. When finally it did, while I was in Vienna, I ought in good sense to have abandoned the idea, according to the advice of several Viennese who seemed to know what they were talking about. "Don't go to Prague," they told me. "It's a city of pedants, where people admire the works only of dead composers. It's true that the Bohemians are fine musicians, but in the manner of professors and schoolmasters: they hate anything new, and you will probably not get along at all well with them."
>
> So, by the time I had made up my mind to forego this trip, someone brought me a copy of the *Gazette musicale de Prague* containing three long articles about my *King Lear* Overture. I got them translated, and, far from finding the malevolent disposition and pedantry that my Viennese friends had attributed to the Bohemians, I saw with delight that this critic possessed the opposite qualities in abundance. The author, Dr. Ambros, seemed to me to combine genuine erudition with sound judgement and vivid imagination. I wrote to thank him and to raise with him my misgivings about how his compatriots might react to me. His reply left me with no doubts and confirmed my resolve to visit Prague. . . .
>
> My friends in Vienna spoke bluntly when they saw that I had made up my mind to go: "The Pragers think they invented Mozart. He's their criterion; they won't listen to a note of your symphonies. They'll show you no mercy!" and so on.

1

But Dr. Ambros had given me confidence, and this time nothing could shake it. Despite the scoffers' gloomy forebodings, I went.[1]

Berlioz is in error concerning Ambros's three-part review of the *King Lear* Overture. It appeared not in Prague, but in Vienna. This is but one of many fictions and lapses we shall encounter in the writings of Berlioz, Hanslick, and others concerning Berlioz's visit to Prague.

August Wilhelm Ambros and Eduard Hanslick were among Berlioz's most enthusiastic votaries in Prague. I quote from one of Hanlick's several descriptions of Ambros in his autobiography:

When I first met Ambros . . . he was a Doctor of Laws and an official in the Ministry of Finance, just as I became a few years later. Like me, he was keener on music than on jurisprudence; neither of us joined the civil service because we were enamoured of it, but the career of a bureaucrat was the fate of many young men in Austria during the period immediately preceding the revolutionary year 1848.[2] In addition, Ambros engaged in reviewing music for the thrice-weekly journal *Bohemia*. His easy-going friendliness made me, a mere student almost a decade younger than he, very proud and happy. For some years my pleasure in all the important musical performances in Prague was doubled and trebled because I heard them with Ambros.

A small, intimate circle of friends, of which Ambros was the central figure, met regularly for four-hand piano playing,[3] discussion, and coffee. Ambros dignified our little gatherings with the name "Davidsbündeleien"[4] in imitation of Robert Schumann's Davidsbündler in Leipzig, a group of musical modernists founded more in Schumann's

---

[1] Hector Berlioz, *Mémoires*, ed. Pierre Citron, 2 vols. (Paris: Garnier-Flammarion, 1969), vol. 2, pp. 215–16. All excerpts in the present volume of Berlioz's *Mémoires* have been translated from this edition.

[2] In March 1848 there were uprisings in Budapest, Prague and Vienna. Historians of the Habsburg empire apply the term "Vormärz" to the eight or ten years preceding those events.

[3] Presumably of compositions by such moderns as Hector Berlioz, Niels Gade, Felix Mendelssohn and Robert Schumann.

[4] Ambrosian punning on derivatives of the German word *Bund*. "Davidsbündler" meant something like "league of David"; "*ein Bündel*" means "a bundle" or "a bunch"; "*Bündelei*" is vernacular for "conspiring" or "plotting."

imagination than in reality. Ambros assumed the name "Flamin,[5] the Last of the Davidsbündler"; the youngest of us, J.E. Hock (a very fine pianist and music teacher), Ambros named "Benjamin." Joseph Heller, a composer and finance official, he called "Obolus"; the music critic Ulm was "Barnabus," my humble self was "Renatus," and so it went. . . .[6]

To know Ambros only from his writings and not from personal association with him was to know only half of this highly gifted, original, always cheerful and good-natured personality. He was a talent, or rather a collection of talents, of a remarkable kind: competent musician and excellent sketcher, at home equally in literature and the law.[7]

The Davidsbündler are important to my narrative because it was in their midst that the scheme to bring Berlioz to Prague was hatched. The Davids hoped he would help them shatter the complacency of the musical philistines (i.e. conservatives) of that city, as the following excerpt from Hanslick's autobiography suggests:

> Until 1846, the concert repertoire in Prague was in a rut typical of the time, but in January of that year Hector Berlioz came and changed all that. Scarcely anyone there had ever heard the name of Berlioz except for our little group. Robert Schumann's essays in the *Neue Zeitschrift für Musik*[8] were our bible, and for some time we had been full of excitement over the brilliant Frenchman. We were predisposed in his favour by the

---

[5] "Flamin" is the name of a character in *Hesperus*, a novel by Jean Paul, i.e. J.P.F. Richter (1763–1825), author of a series of immensely popular German novels. Some of the Prague Davidsbündler, notably Flamin, Obolus and Renatus, used their Davidsbündler names as pseudonyms long after their *Bund* ceased to exist.

[6] Franz Balthazar Ulm (1810–1881) wrote reviews and other articles for *Bohemia* for thirty-two years. He composed many Czech and German songs, and a German opera of which not even the title survives. I have no more information than Hanslick provides concerning pianist and music teacher J.E. Hock and composer and finance official (*Finanzrat*) Joseph Heller.

[7] Eduard Hanslick, *Aus meinem Leben*, 2 vols. (Berlin: Allgemeiner Verein für Deutsche Litteratur, 1894), vol. 1, pp. 41–42.

[8] Robert Schumann, "'Aus dem Leben eines Künstlers,' Phantastische Symphonie in 5 Abtheilungen von Hector Berlioz," *Neue Zeitschrift für Musik*, six instalments beginning vol. 3, no. 1 (3 July 1835), p. 1. There is an English translation by Edward T. Cone in Edward T. Cone, *Hector Berlioz Fantastic Symphony: An Authoritative Score, Historical Background, Analysis, Views and Comments* (New York: Norton, 1971), pp. 220–48.

enthusiastic reviews of his music by Schumann, R. Griepenkerl,[9] and Dr. Becher,[10] and the descriptions of him by Heine.[11] Of Berlioz's compositions we had only the four-hand arrangement of the *King Lear* Overture,[12] and Liszt's transcription for piano solo of the *Symphonie fantastique*,[13] both of which we pounded out indefatigably.[14]

It is one of the most perplexing features of our story that Hanslick nowhere mentions a review he wrote of a concert in Prague featuring Berlioz's *King Lear* Overture.[15] This performance was the first anywhere in Austria of any work by Hector Berlioz, for which reason alone it must have aroused considerable interest. The concert was held in the Platteissaal[16] on 9 March 1845. It was Ambros's review of it that prompted Berlioz to write him and seek his advice about going to Prague. As we have seen, Ambros wrote for the journal *Bohemia*, but on

---

[9] Wolfgang Robert Griepenkerl, *Ritter Berlioz in Braunschweig: Zur Charakteristik dieses Tondichters* (Brunswick: E. Leibrock, 1843).

[10] Dr. A.J. Becher, "Über Hektor Berlioz," *Wiener Allgemeine Musik-Zeitung*, three instalments beginning no. 144 (2 December 1845), p. 573.

[11] Heinrich Heine, "Zehnter Brief," *Stuttgart/Tübingen Allgemeine Theater-Revue*, vol. 3 (1837), pp. 239–40. There is an English translation by F.H. Martens in O.G. Sonneck, "Heinrich Heine's Musical Feuilletons," *The Musical Quarterly*, vol. 8, no. 2 (April 1972), pp. 286–87. Heinrich Heine (1797–1856), German poet and essayist, lived in Paris from 1831 until his death. He was a friend of Berlioz.

[12] Hector Berlioz, arr. J.A. Leibrock (piano four hands), *Le roi Lear* (*King Lear* Overture), op. 4 (Paris: S. Richault, 1843).

[13] Hector Berlioz, arr. Franz Liszt (piano solo), *Grande symphonie fantastique*, op. 14 (Paris: M. Schlesinger, 1843).

[14] Hanslick, *Leben*, vol. 1, p. 56.

[15] Eduard Hanslick [here "Ed–d."], Zweites Konzert des Konservatoriums am 9. März," *Prag*, no. 41 (12 March 1845), pp. 162–63. Chapter II of the present volume consists mainly of a translation of this review. Dr. Jitka Ludvová has brought to my attention a letter from Hanslick to his friend Robert Zimmermann in Vienna dated 8 March 1845. Hanslick here discusses his journalistic activities, but does not mention the *King Lear* performance (9 March) or his reviewing of it. (The letter is in the collection of the National Library in Prague.)

[16] Palais Platteis (sometimes "Platteiß") is in the Old Town of Prague. It is named after its sixteenth-century owners, the family Plateys von Plattenstein, but the structure is originally Gothic, with portions of the early fortifications of Prague in its foundations. In the nineteenth century the Platteissaal contained a display of wax figures, and was used by the Prague Conservatory as a concert hall. Franz Liszt stayed it the Palais Platteis in 1840 and again in 1846; a plaque commemorates these visits. See Hugo Rokyta, *Die Böhmischen Länder* (Salzburg: St. Peter, 1970), p. 29.

this occasion his review was published in *Wiener Allgemeine Musik-Zeitung*. The review of the *King Lear* Overture in *Bohemia* was written by one of that journal's editors, Bernhard Gutt, who wrote:

> I confess that I am at a loss what to say about Berlioz's *King Lear* Overture, because I have no capacity for this music; I did not understand it at all. Even someone who has grasped the marvellous structures of the latest works of Beethoven, the loftiest flights of his titanic genius, will occasionally find something not altogether clear among this composer's profoundest utterances, and this despite the fact that it is precisely in these greatest of all musical works that lapses into unclarity are least likely to occur. In the earlier keyboard pieces of Robert Schumann one could, if one took the trouble, find a sort of method in the madness and, underlying it, a healthy kernel of music which now (Schumann's whimsicality aside) has blossomed quite beautifully. But I cannot regard Berlioz's overture as music, because it lacks the singing soul of music, its harmonically and rhythmically articulated body. I strove in vain to discover a content in this instrumental uproar.
>
> This opinion I submit with misgivings, since friends of mine for whose musical judgement I have the highest regard insist that, although nobody could be expected to grasp the overture as a whole, in its details it has an unspecified, emergent greatness, a certain inspired, ineffable Something.
>
> There is nothing I can do about my incapacity to grasp Berlioz's music except resign myself to this shortcoming. Some people have praised the brilliant orchestration, full of effects as it is. But I am equally incapable of grasping the idea of orchestration for its own sake, in and for itself. What is it, after all, that is orchestrated?[17]

Regarding the character of Johann Friedrich Kittl (1806–1868), who conducted the Conservatory Orchestra on this occasion, Berlioz and Hanslick have left contrasting views on record. Berlioz wrote:

> The Prague Conservatory is directed by a talented composer full of love for the art of music, active, ardent, indefatigable, severe on occasion, lavish with praise when it is deserved—and young! That's Monsieur

---

[17] Bernhard Gutt [here "B. Gutt"], "Zweites Concert des Conservatoriums (Beschluß)," *Bohemia*, vol. 18, no. 31 (14 March 1845), n.p. Gutt's brief career is sketched below, p. 110.

Kittl. They could easily have found some ponderous mediocrity hallowed by his years (for there are some of these even in Bohemia), and assigned to him the task of paralysing, little by little, the musical life of Prague. But not so. On the contrary, they appointed Monsieur Kittl, hence music lives and moves and grows in Prague. Obviously the members of the committee that made such a choice were suffering from an aberration, or else were people with hearts and minds.[18]

Something like that appears to have been the generally accepted opinion of Kittl as Director of the Prague Conservatory, but Hanslick, writing decades later, remembered him not in the same light:

The leading figure in the concert life of Prague in the mid-forties was an ambitious and talented man named Johann Friedrich Kittl. He had been a pupil of Tomaschek,[19] but due to a severe clash of personalities they became bitter enemies, so much so that Tomaschek would not go to any concert at which a piece by Kittl was to be played. A composer of undeniable talent, Kittl in real life was without manly dignity, being sycophantic, petty, and conceited. His external appearance was in accord with this: he was a fat young man with a greasy double chin and nondescript features. The darling of the aristocracy, especially of the women, he was through their influence appointed at an early age to the position of Director of the Conservatory, successor to that grand old pedant Dionys Weber. Kittl soon demonstrated, however, that youth is no obstacle to a person in such a position; indeed, in important matters it is an advantage. So well did he train his young musicians that the Conservatory concerts, at which the orchestra was made up exclusively of professors and pupils of the institution, received a great impetus under his leadership: the orchestra showed itself to be a match for the most difficult assignments. Berlioz, who certainly handed them the hardest nuts to crack, gave the orchestra a glowing commendation. One of Kittl's main achievements was to revive and expand the concert repertoire by offering the best of recent compositions. Orchestral works by Schumann, Mendelssohn, and Gade were performed in Prague, and very well performed at that, long before anyone even thought of doing

---

[18] Berlioz, *Mémoires*, vol. 2, p. 226.
[19] Wenzel Johann Tomaschek (1774–1850) taught several of the most distinguished Bohemian musicians of his time, including Friedrich Kittl and Eduard Hanslick. There is more to come about Tomaschek.

Fig. 2. JOHANN FRIEDRICH KITTL

"... a fat young man with a greasy double chin and nondescript features."

them in Vienna; likewise most operas of Weber, Marschner, Lortzing, and Wagner.[20]

Kittl's performance of the *King Lear* Overture is the starting point for purposes of this narrative. It sparked the journalistic controversy in Prague that prepared the way for Berlioz's reception there. As we have seen, it prompted the essay by Ambros which in turn caught Berlioz's attention in Vienna and inspired him to initiate the correspondence with Ambros which resulted in the events I describe in this book.

This essay by Ambros, like all his writings, is virtually untranslatable, so full is it of literary gewgaws of one kind or another, supposedly in imitation of Jean Paul, for whose writings Ambros never lost his youthful enthusiasm. Hanslick wrote of Ambros:

> He talked the way he wrote, and wrote the way he was: indifferent to form, invariably full of witticisms and imagery, erudite, at one and the same time both polyhistor and improvisator. His bubbling rhetoric might appeal to one person, his opulent style to another, but certainly nobody who heard or read him was bored by him.[21]
>
> Ambros was so devoted to the writings of Jean Paul that he was never able to write in any other than the Paulian manner. . . . Ideas popped into his head like angry fleas, all in a jumble, as Heine said of Jean Paul himself.[22] Ambros never wrote a line in a state of calm, measured enlightenment, without humorous asides, without good and bad jokes, images, and hyperbole. Jean Paul could not pass along his poetic genius to our friend; but he could and did ruin his style.[23]

Ambros was aware of his shortcomings. He once remarked that his pen was like a runaway locomotive in that no amount of braking and

[20] Hanslick, *Leben*, vol. 1, pp. 62–63. Among Kittl's compositions is an opera, *Die Franzosen vor Nizza*, for which the libretto was written by Kittl's friend Richard Wagner.

[21] Hanslick, *Leben*, vol. 1, p. 43.

[22] "In allen Richtungen hüpfen dabey seine Witze, die Flöhe seines erhitzten Geistes." Heinrich Heine, ed. Manfred Windfuhr et al., *Historische-Kritische Gesamtausgabe der Werke*, 15 vols. (Hamburg: Hoffmann & Campe, 1980), vol. 8/1, p. 220.

[23] Hanslick, *Leben*, vol. 1, p. 49. Hanslick continues: "My favourite humorist was Dickens. I have him to thank for more pleasant hours than the author of *Titan* [i.e. Jean Paul]. Even now, Dickens cheers many a quiet evening for me. I have never gone back to Jean Paul." Hanslick's essay "Ritter Berlioz in Prague" is one of his most Jean-Paulian writings; it is evident that this influence was indirect by way of Robert Schumann, who cheerfully acknowledged the influence of Jean Paul upon his own prose.

Fig. 3. August Wilhelm Ambros
"Ideas popped into his head like angry fleas. . . ."

throttling could bring it under control.[24] This will be evident from the following excerpt from the essay on Berlioz's *King Lear* Overture signed "August Wilhelm Ambros, Doctor of Laws, of Prague":

> Any phenomenon concerning which all three of the ancient Roman legal formulae *absolvo, condemno,* and *non liquet*[25] are not merely pronounced, but shouted from the rooftops, deserves notice, the more so if it is at the same time being hotly debated. In the musical world, Berlioz is such a phenomenon. On the one side we hear "Halleluia!" and on the other "Stone him!"; here he is proclaimed a heaven-sent genius, there the title of lunatic is bestowed upon him in fee simple. Some people hear in his music the singing of angels and the roll of thunder, others nothing but a cacophonous din.
>
> The *Neue Zeitschrift für Musik* of Leipzig, especially in its earlier years, was a veritable arena for this kind of jousting. Lobe from Weimar and Gottschalk Wedel (actually Wilhelm von Waldbrühl), both of them thoroughly well informed on artistic matters and both men of the most honest convictions, had at each other in an especially hard fought duel. Concerning Berlioz's *Francs-Juges* Overture, Lobe wrote a so-called "open letter" to Berlioz which would have been an ode but for the lack of alcaic or sapphic metre.[26] In riposte, Wedel turned up as *advocatus diaboli* against Lobe's canonization of Berlioz, in an open letter to German music lovers.[27] Indeed, to this otherwise gentle soul the mere mention of Berlioz's name was like a red flag to a bull. By far the majority of listeners and critics eventually pronounced the *non liquet* and admitted that they did not understand this music, thereby disqualifying themselves as judges on grounds of incompetence instead of, like the others, disqualifying Berlioz's music, i.e. anathematizing it.

---

[24]August Wilhelm Ambros [here "Flamin, der letzte Davidsbündler"], "Händel's 'Messias,' angeführt am 23. Dezember von Prager Tonkünstlervereine," *Bohemia*, vol. 19, no. 196 (31 December 1846), n.p. The reader will recall that the big event of the previous year in Prague was the opening of the railway line connecting Vienna and Prague.

[25] "Acquittal," "condemnation," and "no verdict" respectively.

[26]J.C. Lobe, 'Sendschreiben an Herrn Hector Berlioz in Paris," *Neue Zeitschrift für Musik*, vol. 6, no. 37 (9 May 1837), pp. 147–49.

[27] Gottschalk Wedel [A.W.F. von Zuccalmaglio], "Sendschreiben an die deutschen Tonkundigen," *Neue Zeitschrift für Musik*, vol. 7, no. 47 (12 December 1837), pp. 185–87; no. 49 (19 December 1837), pp. 193–94; no. 50 (22 December 1837), pp. 197–99.

We who live in the various regions of Blessed Austria[28] looked upon all these alarums and excursions with perfect equanimity. "Let them brawl and break their heads," we said, "we can afford to be complacent[29] and point serenely to Gluck, Haydn, Mozart and Beethoven, and claim them for our own."[30] We were curious about what was going on, as who would not be? Of Berlioz's compositions no scores were to be had, so perforce we got by with the music in pauper's attire, that is to say in piano arrangements, in which the original, even if it be a blazing image of the sun, is captured, as it were, in so many mirrors and reflected from one to another so many times that it fades into a pale lunar disk. At first we went along with the *non liquet* faction.

Then, in 1843, Berlioz undertook his much-publicized musical journey to Germany. His arrival was reported in the journals almost as if it were an outbreak of cholera; one cynic put it that Berlioz was an appendix to the grievous misfortunes of the year 1842. Now the hullabaloo was worse than ever. While Herr Griepenkerl led the way carrying whole forests of laurel for his hero in the pamphlet *Ritter Berlioz in Braunschweig*,[31] just about the whole pack of newspapers were tentatively snapping at Berlioz's heels. Almost all their discourses boiled down to little more than Gutzkow's remark that Berlioz wants to laugh, weep, and die like Beethoven, only his laughing is grinning, his weeping is whining, and his dying is caricature.[32]

Then it was reported that Berlioz was in Dresden. Now, surely, he would come to us, and we would see and hear for ourselves. But lo! He came not! A few people thought he was shying away from the musical orthodoxy of Prague; others remembered that Vienna is the wall against which all the losers pound their heads, and that just as once the Ottoman hordes were prevented by Vienna from advancing further,

---

[28] Ambros relied on his readers to recognize this ancient Austrian paraphrase based on Ovid: "Bella gerant alii! Tu, felix Austria, nube! Nam quae Mars aliis, dat tibi regna Venus" ("Others wage war, but you, Blessed Austria, engage in matrimony—for their allegiance is to Mars, yours to Venus"). Reference is to Austria's tradition of expansion more by means of advantageous royal marriages than by military adventures. See Franz Freiherr von Lipperheide, *Spruchwörterbuch*, 4th ed. (Berlin: Haude & Spenersche, 1962), p. 672.

[29] Literally "our lambkins are in the byre." It seemed advisable to replace this Jean-Paulian "flea" with a loose paraphrase.

[30] We do well to remind ourselves occasionally that neither Gluck nor Haydn nor Mozart nor Beethoven was Austrian by birth.

[31] See note 9 above.

[32] Karl Gutzkow, *Briefe aus Paris*, 2 parts (Leipzig: Brockhaus, 1842), part 2, p. 32.

etc., etc. At any rate, Berlioz went away without having come to us, and so we were left with but a dim, fuzzy impression of his artistic personality in the form of gigantic outlines of a fabulous monster; he was for us a kind of Bow Wow and Mumbo Jumbo, a monstrosity that with mammoth's lumbering tread tramples all the seeds and plants to a pulp, before whose musical orgies every musically right-thinking soul makes the sign of the cross.

All that changed on the ninth day of March, 1845.

On that day Prague had the distinction of being the first city in Austria to mount a public performance of a work by Berlioz. The Director of the Conservatory, Herr Kittl, obtained a copy of the score, and, in the program of the second Conservatory concert on March 9th, we Pragers got to hear the *King Lear* Overture in orchestral performance. Kittl stepped in front of his young and enthusiastic troops and raised his baton, that sceptre from Wonderland, the magic wand that (as the Thessalian sorceress the moon)[33] had the power to bring down an unknown paradise to earth, though certainly not without raising an occasional satanic grimace from below.

The Overture began.

Your scribe wished very much that some daguerreotypist had been secretly at work there, facing the audience (the more so since your scribe's countenance would thereby have preserved for posterity); the overture lasted ten or twelve minutes, during which time the audience sat stunned, as motionless as any daguerreotypist could have wished. We would then have had a picture with the title "How a musically cultivated audience looks upon first hearing Berlioz."

The faces of the listeners fell into three categories: (*a*) astonished; (*b*) fascinated; (*c*) derisive.

The first category was the most numerous. Actually, a touch of astonishment ran across all the faces, while, *vice versa*, the astonished ones had just a touch of either fascination or derision. At the end the consensus was that the work was very strange, but very brilliant and moving.

Admittedly this overture is harder to digest than toadstool salad; it is rather like a salad made of oakwood pickled with rocks and the like. Admittedly there are things in it about which one could repeat Lear's

---

[33] J.W. von Goethe, *Faust*, part 2, act 2, scenes "Am obern Peneios, wie zuvor" and "Felsbuchten des Ägäischen Meers."

words: "You will say they are Persian attire; but let them be changed."[34] But that the overture not only as a whole conveys the spirit of Shakespeare's tragedy marvellously, but in its details teems with strokes of sublime genius; that the inner power of the work is greater than the external power of its instrumental mass; that it is a work in which intellect, blazing inspiration, and a profound, sublime temperament reach out to touch one another—all this only he could fail to appreciate whose musical criteria have been firmly drawn up in advance, and who measures everything in inches and straight lines.[35]

Ambros's review of the *King Lear* Overture continues in this vein at some length. Hector Berlioz, as we saw at the beginning of this chapter, formed on the basis of his reading of the review the opinion that Ambros "combined genuine erudition with sound judgement and vivid imagination." It is not hard to see why.

Three of the writers mentioned by Ambros were in their own ways as colourful as Ambros himself: Lobe, Wedel, and Gutzkow. "Gottschalk Wedel" and "Dorfküster A.W. von Waldbrühl" are pseudonyms of Anton Wilhelm Fiorentin von Zuccalmaglio, who perhaps had better reason than some other writers to use pseudonyms. The ferocity of his exchange with Johann Christian Lobe over Berlioz in Robert Schumann's *Neue Zeitschrift für Musik* in 1837 is hardly exaggerated by Ambros. As for Karl Gutzkow, his word-portrait of Hector Berlioz in his *Briefe aus Paris* (1842)[36] is more Jean-Paulian than anything in the *King Lear* review by Ambros.

---

[34] William Shakespeare, *King Lear*, III, vi.

[35] August Wilhelm Ambros [here "Jur. Dr. August Wilhelm Ambros aus Prag"], "Die Ouvertüre zu Shakespeare's 'König Lear' von Hektor Berlioz," *Wiener Allgemeine Musik-Zeitung*, three instalments beginning vol. 5, no. 120 (7 October 1845), p. 477.

In July 1845, under the heading "Aus Prag," a few lines appeared about the *King Lear* Overture in Robert Schumann's *Neue Zeitschrift für Musik* over the signature "– 29 –". In the same journal, vol. 26, no. 6 (18 January 1847), pp. 22–23, "– 29 –" unmasks: he is "Dr. August Ambros." Here is what Ambros as "– 29 –" says about the *King Lear* Overture: "I consider it a work well shaped along traditional lines, rich in beautiful ideas, in which greatness and a certain tragic tendency are also evident, but also monstrosities and hideous extravagances. For me it stands in relation to, say, Mendelssohn's 'Die schöne Melusine' as a gnarled oaken stump to a vase full of lilies in full bloom." August Wilhelm Ambros [here "– 29 –"], "Aus Prag," *Neue Zeitschrift für Musik*, vol. 23, no. 1 (1 July 1845), p. 3.

[36] See note 32 above.

Lobe and Wedel figure in the literary background to Hanslick's encounter with Berlioz in 1846. They are among the many writers in German on music and music theory of the period 1750–1850. That hundred years witnessed an extraordinary proliferation of books and journals in German on those topics, most of them displaying a passion for music quite incomprehensible to readers of our time. In the city of Berlin alone, during the decade 1747–57, thirty-one titles of new books and journals on musical theory and criticism appeared, to a total of more than five thousand pages.[37]

Comparable figures might be produced for other German cities and other decades during this remarkable hundred years, at the end of which appeared Eduard Hanslick's *Vom Musikalisch-Schönen* (1854).[38] In this little book Hanslick, not yet aged thirty, took a firm stand against the majority of his predecessors—indeed, against the view of music he had shared with them as late as 1846. This is the view that the defining purpose of music is to express or arouse feelings, or to portray extramusical objects and situations capable of arousing them. In his writings of the decade 1845–54 we can observe Hanslick gradually abandoning the "feeling-theory" (as he calls it), and forging his own theory as we find it expounded in *Vom Musikalisch-Schönen*. We discuss some aspects of this theory in our concluding chapter.

A.W. Ambros shows his allegiance to the feeling-theory where he says in his review that Berlioz's *King Lear* Overture "conveys the spirit of Shakespeare's tragedy marvellously." Hanslick, in his own review of the same work, is more cautious on this point, as we shall see in the next chapter. He merely refers to an "undeniably splendid element that blows upon us like the night air off that ghastly heath and recalls to mind the madness of the senile King in all its dreadful sublimity."[39]

---

[37] Hans-Günther Ottenburg, ed., *Der critische Musicus an der Spree* (Leipzig: Reclam, 1984), p. 7.

[38] Eduard Hanslick, *Vom Musikalisch-Schönen* (Leipzig: Weigl, 1854).

[39] See below, p. 21. Nevertheless we have here an illustration of Hanslick's subsequent change of view regarding the music of Berlioz. I quote from my translation of Hanslick's book: "The splendid overture of Berlioz, in itself, has no more to do with the mental image we have of King Lear than has a Strauss waltz. . . . We are compelled by a particular title to compare the piece with an object outside it and to evaluate the piece by an extramusical criterion." Eduard Hanslick, trans. Geoffrey Payzant, *On the Musically Beautiful* (Indianapolis: Hackett, 1986), p. 75.

When we read those remarks we are prompted to ask: What impression must their authors have had of Shakespeare's *King Lear* that they would think Berlioz's music "conveys the spirit" of the drama, or "recalls to mind the madness of the senile King"? Were they familiar with *King Lear* in English? So far as I am able to tell, Hanslick had little use of that language, Ambros almost none at all. As educated young men of their time and place, however, both were undoubtedly familiar with *König Lear* in the Baudissin translation.[40]

Hanslick tells of an occasion on which he, still a teenager, attended a performance of *König Lear*. It is a poignant story. I retell it here because it helps fill in the social and political background to our narrative of Hanslick and Berlioz in Prague.

At some time in the 1860s, in Vienna, Hanslick met socially an actor whom he had admired in various performances in the Burgtheater in that city. The actor's name was Karl La Roche. In the course of their conversation, Hanslick mentioned to La Roche that he had greatly admired him in the title role of *König Lear*. "Impossible," snapped the actor, "I have never played Lear." With due apology Hanslick insisted that it was in the summer of 1843 or 1844 that he had seen La Roche in *König Lear*. La Roche capitulated, and confessed that he had always wanted to play Lear, but that for political reasons he did not dare to do so in Vienna; he played the role only once, "in the provinces," i.e. in Prague, just as Hanslick had said.

During those Vormärz[41] years, all publications and public performances were censored by the imperial authorities. To represent on stage a monarch brought to a bad end by members of his own family would have been considered seditious and inflammatory.

Hanslick ends his vignette of La Roche with the remark that in those days Shakespeare's *König Lear* was performed in Prague in a mutilated version with a happy ending.[42]

* * * * *

---

[40] Wolf Heinrich Graf Baudissin (1789–1878) was a German government official who wrote translations as an avocation. He contributed thirteen translations to the Schlegel-Tieck German editions of Shakespeare (1825–33), including *König Lear*.
[41] See note 2 above.
[42] Hanslick, *Leben*, vol. 1, p. 222. There exists an edition of Shakespeare's *König Lear* "adapted" (*eingerichtet*) specifically for performance in the Royal and Imperial Court

In the weeks before Berlioz left Vienna for Prague there must have been a flurry of activity in both cities in preparation for the journey and the visit. Not all of the arrangements in Prague could have been made by Ambros, since as a minor government official and a part-time music reviewer he would not have been able to approach directly some of the men of exalted station upon whom the success of Berlioz's visit would depend. When it came to the matter of arranging for the assistance of a local orchestra, it was the famous composer himself who had to take the initiative, no doubt at Ambros's suggestion. Berlioz wrote:

> To His Excellency Count Nostitz
> I intend to depart soon for Prague in order to perform there a few of my compositions. I take the liberty of asking if you would be so kind as to obtain for me the participation of the Prague Conservatory Orchestra, of whose excellence everyone speaks. I would be grateful for such a favour, and much indebted to you for it.
>
> Please excuse my presuming to approach you in this matter without having had the honour of your acquaintance, and accept the respectful regards of your faithful servant
>
> H. Berlioz
Vienna, January 9th, 1846[43]

Albert Count Nostitz (1807–1871) was a statesman, businessman, and patron of the arts in Prague. His father was one of the founders of the Prague Conservatory in 1810, and his grandfather provided the funds to design and build the Ständetheater as a gift to his fellow citizens in Prague (it first opened to the public in 1783). In the year of Berlioz's visit

---

Theatre (Burgtheater) in Vienna by C.A. West (Vienna: Wallishauser, 1841). Lear and Cordelia survive, are reunited, and live happily ever after. "C.A. West" is a pseudonym of Joseph Schreivogel. He was secretary and dramaturge in the Burgtheater from 1814 until his death in 1832.

[43] From a facsimile in Rudolf Freiherr Procházka, *Das romantische Musik-Prag: Charakterbilder* (Saaz i.B.: Verlag Dr. H. Erben, 1914), between pp. 32 and 33. See also the Foreword (n.p.), which states that the original of this letter is in the Archives of the Prague Conservatory. Berlioz's letter of 9 January 1846 is mentioned in Johann Branberger, trans. Emil Bezecný, *Das Konservatorium für Musik in Prag zur 100-Jahrfeier der Gründung im Auftrage des Vereines zur Berförderung der Tonkunst in Böhmen, mit Benützung der Denkschrift von Dr. A.W. Ambros vom Jahre 1858* (Prague: Verlag des Vereines zur Beförderung der Tonkunst in Böhmen, 1911), p. 252. It is not to be found in the *Correspondance Générale* (see note 45 below).

to Prague, Nostitz was Referent of the Society for the Advancement of Music in Bohemia, the Conservatory's parent organization.

The title "Referent" does not readily translate into English, but the holder of that office stood second only to the President in the Society's organization; Nostitz was elected President in 1850, and held that office until his death twenty-one years later, at which time he was mourned as "Father of the Conservatory."[44]

Director Kittl (he was appointed in 1843) reported to the President and Executive of the Society. Though responsible for the day-to-day administration of the Conservatory, he could not have been expected to make policy decisions such as whether to allow the Conservatory's own orchestra to perform under a visiting conductor for that conductor's own benefit. This, I suppose, is why Berlioz wrote to Nostitz and not to Kittl from Vienna on 9 January 1846 as above.[45]

After several false starts (about which more in due course) Hector Berlioz left Vienna by train for Prague on or about 12 January 1846.

---

[44] Details in my account of Nostitz come from Constant von Wurzbach, *Biographisches Lexikon des Kaiserthums Oesterreich*, 60 vols. (Vienna: k.-k. Hof- und Staatsdrukerei, 1856–91), s.v. "Nostitz, Graf Albert von," and Branberger, *Das Konservatorium für Musik in Prag. . .*, which incorporates a history of the Prague Conservatory written by A.W. Ambros and was first published in 1858 in celebration of the Conservatory's fiftieth anniversary.

[45] Berlioz's *Correspondance Générale* lists a letter from Berlioz to Kittl dated 11 January 1846, but of this letter's content there appears to be no record. Hector Berlioz, ed. Pierre Citron, *Correspondance Générale*, 4 vols. (Paris: Flammarion, 1972), vol. 3, p. 305. In the present volume, all translations from Berlioz's correspondence (with the exception of the 9 January 1846 letter to Nostitz) are made from this edition.

II

King Lear Overture: Review by "Ed–d."

EDUARD HANSLICK'S REVIEW of the *King Lear* Overture by Hector Berlioz is so important for us that it requires a chapter to itself, albeit a brief one. This review marks an important stage in Hanslick's development as musical theorist and critic. It is noticeably at odds in important respects with his essay "Ritter Berlioz in Prague," which appeared the following year; as already mentioned, the performance on which it reports was the first of any work by Berlioz anywhere in Austria, and hence the starting point of our narrative.

The review appeared in *Prag: Beiblätter zu "Ost und West,"* the issue of 12 March 1845,[1] three days after the *King Lear* Overture was performed in the Platteissaal. Bernhard Gutt's review of the overture appeared in *Bohemia* on 14 March; Ambros's review did not appear in the *Wiener Allgemeine Musik-Zeitung* until October of the same year.

At the time he wrote this review, Eduard Hanslick was a student at Prague University and not yet aged twenty-one. His affectation of bearded authority may be endearing to some readers, irritating to others. So far as I know, this review has been neither reprinted in German nor published in translation.

We conclude this chapter with Eduard Hanslick's review.

> Is there anyone who was not looking forward with the highest expectations to the concert whose announcement promised us Berlioz's *King*

---

[1] In the literature about Hanslick's youth in Prague there is confusion between the parent journal *Ost und West: Blätter für Kunst, Literatur und geselliges Leben* (hereinafter *Ost und West*), and its supplement *Prag: Beiblätter zu "Ost und West."* In the hope of reducing the confusion I shall refer to the latter merely as *Prag*. *Ost und West* published *Prag* from 1841 to the end of 1845. All Hanslick's reviews of the years 1844 and 1845 appeared in *Prag*, with the signature "Ed–d." His essay "Ritter Berlioz in Prague" appeared in *Ost und West* in January 1846 signed "Eduard Hanslik." (My translation of this essay constitutes Chapter IV below.)

Fig. 4. RITTER BERLIOZ in Vienna, 1845.

Lear Overture? At long last, it would be granted to us Pragers to become acquainted with Berlioz, at whom heretofore we could only gaze in wonder from afar, the Great Unknown. One still remembers what a mighty rejoicing the *Neue Zeitschrift für Musik* of Leipzig set up a few years ago over the Frenchman, and how Robert Schumann hailed him as the new musical Messiah.[2] Your reviewer is not the only person who at that time analysed Berlioz's *Symphonie fantastique* by the sweat of his brow, and who came to the conclusion that it was indeed fantastic.[3]

In Berlioz's compositions there is always something undeniably novel, something unique. But if, for that reason, we saw in this musical eccentric a rejuvenator of our music, and asserted that Berlioz's compositions must open up a whole new avenue and bring about a revolution in contemporary music, we were much too hasty.[4] We can say that our music, as a matter of historical necessity, will not remain static in its present condition, and we can predict that it will always undergo new developments and upheavals. The history of music shows us how the striving for ever more spontaneous, unrestricted legitimization of the Idea[5] has always been active in music, has smashed the chains that earlier periods wore, and opened new, unexpected directions. In this way, perhaps our descendants will hear music such as has never been dreamed of in our philosophy.

But Berlioz is not the person who will give music a new direction; this only a true Chosen One can do, whom genius has stamped with divine

---

[2] See p. 3, note 8.

[3] Robert Schumann's essay on Berlioz appeared in 1835; Eduard Hanslick was then a lad of ten years, so we may doubt that he at that time analysed the score of the *Symphonie fantastique*, with or without sweat on his brow. There is more such youthful swagger to come in his essay "Ritter Berlioz in Prague." "Ed–d." must have known that his readers were aware of his true identity, hence that he was not the hoary veteran critic he made himself out to be in his *King Lear* review.

[4] Compare these lines with "Ritter Berlioz in Prague," where Hanslick lauds Berlioz as an artist who has opened up new avenues, extended and liberated the laws of musical form, etc.

[5] The view that the law of progress in the arts and in everything else is a matter of historical necessity was a commonplace in German idealistic philosophy and in romantic literary theory at the time Hanslick wrote his review (1845); perhaps he acquired the present version from a secondary Hegelian source. "Legitimization of the Idea" (*Berechtigung der Idee*) could serve as a paraphrase of several formulations by Hegel in the Introduction to his *Aesthetics*. The Hegelian point here is that in every work of art something mental or "ideal" (i.e. the Idea) is embodied, becomes manifest to perception in something physical, and that this external or physical manifestation must be "adequate" to its Idea, and the Idea to its manifestation. The "adequacy" is the "legitimization" of which Hanslick speaks.

consecration. There must come a Gluck if we are to have a new kind of opera, a Beethoven if a new kind of instrumental music. Berlioz has much intelligence and acumen, thorough training, and an all-too-feverish imagination; but for musical inventiveness he possesses little power. He has laboured upon his half-dozen works with indescribable effort, goaded by an equally indescribable ambition. If people are so misled by the strangeness and eccentricity of his works as to consider him a great musical genius, they forget that with Berlioz it is not the tacit urging of genius that prompts in him the unfamiliar, the that-which-never-was: Berlioz pokes around deliberately in the glowing forge of his overheated imagination in search of the monstrous, and often picks out the that-which-never-was precisely *because* it never was.

The *King Lear* Overture confirms all this perfectly. There is much spirit in this work; indeed, an undeniably splendid element that blows upon us like the night air off that ghastly heath, and brings to mind the madness of the senile King in all its dreadful sublimity. Yet the effect is of an extravagance and bizarreness, the workmanship of an unclarity and sloppiness, of which, really, there is no equivalent in all of music. Berlioz feels he has to put something extraordinary into every measure, thus inevitably he often oversteps the critical limit of which the words "du sublime au ridicule il n'y a qu'un pas" warn us. But it is in the nature of the French to pay the least possible attention to precisely this maxim of their very own, although God knows they need to observe it more that anyone. As is well known, Berlioz has made of orchestration the subject of a special, unremitting study;[6] the *King Lear* Overture possesses an abundance of the most extraordinary and ingenious instrumental effects. An example is the place in the introduction where the three trombones have the melody while the other winds rap out the chords in thirty-second notes,[7] and the violins mingle with a curious ascending figure; another example is the truly overwhelming use of trombones and tympani in many places.

Hanslick soon abandoned his allegiance to the law of progress in the arts based upon historical necessity. G.W.F. Hegel, trans. T.M. Knox, *Aesthetics: Lectures on Fine Art*, 2 vols. (Oxford, 1975). The original German text is in G.W.F. Hegel, *Werke*, 19 vols. (Berlin, 1853), vol. 10.

[6] Hector Berlioz, *Grande traité d'instrumentation et d'orchestration moderne* (Paris: Schonenberger, 1843).

[7] Hanslick here refers to the "canto dolce" that appears on p. 7 of the Eulenburg score of the *King Lear* Overture. The notes in question are not thirty-seconds, but sixteenths at six in

Musical philistines and pedants will, in any event, denounce the *King Lear* music as a monstrosity, a product of the most extravagant madness. Yet I firmly maintain that, with all its strangeness, it is worth more than dozens of overtures which can boast of their formal correctness. I have made a point of keeping my judgement concerning Berlioz free of any taint of presumption: I have written it down scrupulously and impartially, according to my best understanding of his music, but at the same time with the firm conviction that only in the future will this (for us) excessively strange phenomenon be properly understood and judged.[8]

---

the time of four. I have not seen the piano four-hand version with which Hanslick was familiar: Hector Berlioz (arr. J.A. Leibrock for piano four hands), *Le roi Lear* (*King Lear* Overture), op. 4. Paris: S. Richault, 1843.

[8] Hanslick [here "Ed–d."], "Zweites Konzert," pp. 162–63. Continued in the succeeding issue, but the continuation does not deal with the *King Lear* Overture.

III

Arrival and First Impressions

ECTOR BERLIOZ ARRIVED at the Staatsbahnhof in Prague on 14 January 1846, having travelled on the recently completed railway (the Nordbahn) from Vienna by way of Olmütz.[1] At last the Pragers would get to see the Bow Wow, the Mumbo Jumbo, the Great Unknown.

Two Davidsbündler were on hand to welcome him, both no doubt in high excitement: Flamin (August Wilhelm Ambros) and Renatus (Eduard Hanslick). Berlioz provides an amusing account of his meeting with them; the reader should keep in mind that Berlioz was not above average height; hence for a "little man" such as Ambros he would have been difficult to spot in the crowd and bustle of a railway platform. Here is Berlioz in a letter to his friend Humbert Ferrand:[2]

> Isn't it pleasant when, a hundred leagues from home, you get off the train in a strange place, to have an unknown friend awaiting you on the platform, who, recognizing from your splendidly distinctive countenance that you are his man, greets you, shakes your hand, and in your own language tells you that all arrangements have been made for you?
>
> That's how it was with Dr. Ambros when I arrived in Prague, except that my splendidly distinctive countenance failed utterly in its effect: he didn't recognize me. On the contrary, it was I who, spotting a little man of lively and benevolent features, and hearing him say in French to his companion "But how am I supposed to recognize Berlioz in this crowd? I've never laid eyes upon him!"—it was I (I repeat) who had the

---

[1] "Hector Berlioz arrived by train the day before yesterday." *Bohemia*, vol. 19, no. 7 (16 January 1846), n.p. The railway line from Vienna to Prague had been completed only a few weeks previously, although it was officially "opened," with much imperial pageantry and speech-making, in August 1845. The Staatsbahnhof (now Praha-střed nádraži) was fewer than ten minutes' walk from the Blue Star Hotel.

[2] Ferrand (1805–1868), a French poet with the pseudonym "Georges Arandas," was a long-time friend and collaborator of Berlioz.

Fig. 5. PRAGUE RAILWAY STATION in 1845.

unimaginable perspicuity to divine that this was Ambros. So I went briskly up to the two of them. "Here I am!" I said.

"Monsieur Berlioz?"

"None other!"

"Excellent! How are you? We are delighted to meet you at last. Let's be on our way. We have an apartment and an orchestra all warmed up for you; we think you'll be pleased with them. But tonight you can relax. Tomorrow we'll get to work!"[3]

So off the four of them went *zum blauen Stern*, to the Blue Star Hotel (as we shall hereinafter call it) close by. Berlioz was accompanied on both his German tours not by his wife, the failed actress Harriet Smithson, but by a failed singer named Marie Recio.[4] This gave rise to an awkward moment during those first few minutes of becoming acquainted in Prague. Hanslick wrote:

> Berlioz came in the company of a fiery-eyed Spanish lady named Mariquita Recio, concerning whom he gave it out that she was his wife. So we could be excused for taking her to be the former actress Miss Smithson, who was known and cherished by us [i.e. the Prague Davidsbündler] from Heine's reports.[5] But when Ambros, upon our first encounter, expressed his pleasure at beholding the prototype of the "double idée fixe" of the *Symphonie fantastique*, namely Miss Smithson, he received a baleful glance from Berlioz and the reply "This is my second wife; Miss Smithson is dead."[6] In truth, his wife was still living

---

[3] Berlioz, *Mémoires*, vol. 2, p. 216. Much of the account by Berlioz of his experiences in Prague was first published in the *Gazette musicale*, subsequently in Berlioz's *Souvenirs de Voyages* and finally in his *Mémoires*. There are variants from one to another; it would not serve the purposes of the present study to go into these. It suffices to cite and translate from a standard text.

[4] There is no mention of a travelling companion in Berlioz's account of his second German tour. In his account of his first he merely says: "But I did not go alone; I had a travelling companion who has come along with me on all my various tours ever since." Berlioz, *Mémoires*, vol. 2, p. 42.

[5] Heine, "Zehnter Brief," pp. 239–40.

[6] Henrietta (or Harriet) Berlioz died 3 March 1854; Berlioz and Marie Recio married 19 October of that year. "Double idée fixe" is Berlioz's own term for the love motive in his *Symphonie fantastique*, a work supposedly inspired by Berlioz's unrequited love for Harriet (*née* Smithson). See Cone, *Berlioz Fantastic Symphony*, pp. 22, 56. A.W. Ambros told the music lovers of Prague that the "subject" (*Gegenstand*) of the *Symphonie fantastique* is Berlioz's first and last love, and still his beloved wife. August Wilhelm Ambros, "Sendschreiben an sämmtliche Musikfreunde Prags," *Prager Zeitung*, no. 11 (18 January 1846), p. 127.

while Berlioz and his Spanish lady were on their travels through Germany and Austria, and she lived on for some time afterwards.[7]

The Blue Star Hotel was in a convenient and expensive location in the Old Town of Prague, across from the Pulverturm (Gunpowder Tower) and not far from the Ständetheater, in which Mozart had enjoyed some of his greatest artistic triumphs. History soon repeated itself in that same theatre for Berlioz.

It was not under the sponsorship of some prelate or aristocrat that Berlioz came to Prague; he was there on his own account. Monsieur le Chevalier Hector Berlioz, however, could not be expected to make do with a modest *Pension* on a side street nobody ever heard of; at whatever cost to himself, he had to cut a figure wherever he went to promote his compositions and himself as conductor. For this purpose, the Blue Star served admirably: Frederick Chopin stayed there in 1829 and 1830, Mikhail Bakunin in 1848; it was there that the treaty between Austria and Prussia was signed in 1866.[8] It was what a later generation would call "a good address."

Presumably Berlioz and Marie Recio brought with them the usual baggage of a couple travelling by train. In addition, a few days later Berlioz's scores and parts for those of his compositions he intended to perform in Prague arrived (by postal wagon, to take advantage of lower freight charges). These were bulky:

> One of the great difficulties of my trip to Germany, and one I could least have foreseen, was the enormous cost of transporting my music. . . . This mass of separate orchestral and choral parts, in manuscript, lithograph, and engraving, was very heavy. I had to arrange for them to follow by postal wagon almost everywhere I went, at great expense.[9]

We can imagine with what consternation the management of the Blue Star Hotel received this shipment of orchestral and choral scores and

---

[7] Hanslick, *Leben*, vol. 1, p. 57.

[8] The Blue Star Hotel was on the Graben (Na příkopě), across from the Pulverturm. A bank now stands on the site.

[9] Berlioz, *Mémoires*, vol. 2, p. 62. Jacques Barzun says that the music weighed five hundred pounds and went by postal wagon for the reason that the fledgling railways were unable to guarantee safe delivery. Jacques Barzun, *Berlioz and the Romantic Century*, 2 vols. (Boston: Little, Brown, 1950), vol. 1, p. 433.

Fig. 6. Opposite the Blue Star Hotel: the PULVERTURM.

parts when eventually it arrived from Vienna: Three symphonies, two overtures, two other orchestral works, a major work for chorus and orchestra (the *Requiem*), and three recently composed pieces for solo voice with orchestral accompaniment. Older members of the hotel staff perhaps remembered Herr Chopin arriving there, sixteen or seventeen years previously, with all his music in a modest satchel. As was being pointed out in some of the journals, Berlioz was a new kind of musician: a soloist whose instrument is the Grand Orchestra. He was the first virtuoso conductor to go on tour to display himself in that capacity.[10] Scores and parts of his works were not yet in the collections of local orchestras, conservatories, and concert societies.

Eduard Hanslick wrote in his autobiography:

> Every day Ambros and I went to collect Berlioz at the Blue Star and go with him to the rehearsals. We were welcome as enthusiastic devotees of his, and, in addition, I made myself useful as interpreter and translator for him. Berlioz did not understand a word of German, and at that time French was in short supply among the musicians of Prague.[11]

We may suppose, accordingly, that on the morning after their arrival in Prague, Berlioz and Recio were met at the hotel by Ambros and Hanslick and were taken on a preliminary reconnaissance of the city. Hanslick had been brought up in a household wherein French was one of the languages in daily use; his mother had an enthusiasm for French literature and saw to it that her children had every opportunity to share her delight in it. Ambros may have had something better than school

---

[10] Katinka Emingerová, trans. "J.H. and J.P.", "Hector Berlioz à Prague," *La Revue française de Prague* (1933), p. 170.

[11] Hanslick, *Leben*, vol. 1, pp. 56–57. There is another version in Eduard Hanslick, *Aus dem Concertsaal: Kritiken und Schilderungen* (Vienna: Braumüller, 1870), pp. 483–84: "A stroke of luck soon brought me into regular contact with the Great Man. As is well known, music is a universal language; but its practitioners stick tenaciously to their national idiom. Berlioz understood not one syllable of German; yet there was much of a musical nature he had to say to people from whom no knowledge of French was to be expected. Since I often functioned in Prague as an interpreter, I soon entered into a degree of closeness to the illustrious composer to which otherwise I would not have been entitled."

French, since his father was an amateur linguist, but even this would not have been adequate for him to carry on in the style of his effervescent chatter in German with his family and friends. Berlioz himself was no mean chatterer, so Hanslick must on occasion have found himself hard-pressed to handle the verbal traffic as the four of them, lively temperaments all, went out to meet musicians and functionaries. Marie Recio was no doubt one of the party, since she had established herself as Berlioz's business manager on tour. Hanslick wrote:

> For the conduct of mundane and business affairs, she, being as tight-fisted with money as he was prodigal, was quite indispensable to her impractical Hector. "How fortunate for Hector that he has me as his wife!" she exclaimed on one occasion when I translated for her the estimates of costs for one of the concerts, slashing them with bold strokes of her pen.[12]

And in another place:

> Señora Mariquita managed the concerts, checked the accounts, mercilessly beat down the fee for triangle and cymbals. She was a kind of worldly Providence, the earthly rose in the heavenly life, a piano arrangement by Madame Vieuxtemps.[13] "It's a good thing for Hector that I'm his wife," she lisped after many a heated negotiation over some account or other—and actually not without justice. If he did not have this dark-eyed Finance Minister, "Hector," guileless and open-handed as a royal heir apparent, would soon have lost all his pocket money and would perhaps have turned up at rehearsal one morning dressed like a Scottish Highlander, lacking essential items of attire.[14]

We turn now to Berlioz's own account of his first impressions of Prague, beginning with the day after his arrival there. Although he mentions neither Marie Recio nor Eduard Hanslick, it can hardly be doubted that both were in the thick of it all. Berlioz compresses the events of the first few days into one, apparently for literary effect. Following this account I shall fill in some details regarding persons and places.

---

[12] Hanslick, *Leben*, vol. 1, p. 57.
[13] Mme Vieuxtemps was wife of violin virtuoso Henri Vieuxtemps. Born Josephine Eder, she was a pupil of Karl Czerny and a famous concert pianist.
[14] Hanslick, *Concertsaal*, p. 485.

On the day after our arrival, after having gone to meet the musical bigwigs of the city, we began making preparations for my first concert [19 January 1846]. But first Ambros introduced me to the director of the Conservatory, Monsieur Kittl; Kittl in turn introduced me to the brothers Škroup . . . and to the concertmaster, Monsieur Mildner. Then we had to meet singers, journalists, and prominent musical patrons.

When all that had been attended to, I asked Ambros to introduce me to the city. "Over there I catch a glimpse of a mountain literally covered with monumental structures, and, as is quite unlike me, I am extremely curious to have a closer look," I said.

"All right, let's go!" said the kind Doctor.

This must be the only occasion on which I did not regret my distress resulting from my exertions in such a climb. (Of course, I exclude Vesuvius, and I have never seen Etna.) Joking aside, it *is* an arduous climb; but that continuous procession of temples, palaces, battlements, steeples, turrets, colonnades, arches, and spacious courtyards! Marvellous! What a view from the top of this mountain embroidered in marble! On one side a forest runs down to a rather extensive plain; on the other a cascade of houses tumbles amidst great clouds of haze into the Moldau, which flows majestically through the city accompanied by the clatter of watermills and various workshops powered by them, and which jumps over a dam imposed upon the river by Bohemian ingenuity to control its direction at this point. The river leaves two [actually three] small islands behind, and loses itself in the distance, meandering through rust-coloured hills which seem to guide it with tender care to the horizon.

"Over there you can see Hunter's Island [l'île des Chasseurs]," my guide told me, "so called, no doubt, because there are no game animals on it. Just beyond it, a bit upstream, you can see Sophie's Island [l'île de Sophie], in the centre of which is Sophie's Concert Hall, where you are going to give your concert, and which is reserved almost exclusively for the meetings of Sophie's Singing Academy."

"And who is this Sophie," I asked, "in whose concert hall, academy, and island I shall have the honour of conducting my concert? Is she some kind of Moldavian nymph? Or the heroine of some romantic legend of which the island is the setting? Or is she just some washerwoman with red, chapped hands, a modern Calypso whose songs and scrubbing paddle once made the welkin ring there?"

Fig. 7. "Over there I catch a glimpse of a mountain literally covered with monumental structures": Hradschin with the Karlsbrücke in the foreground.

"I consider the latter conjecture the more likely," he replied, "but tradition is silent on the question of whether or not her hands were chapped."

"Ah, Doctor, you have the air of someone who has played opposite Sophie in the role of Ulysses! Is there a Eucharis on Calypso's Island? Shall I play the part of Telemachus and go looking for you there?"

In reply the Doctor went red in the face, so it was apparent that I should harp no longer on that string. I never did find out who this Sophie was, this patroness of a singing academy, a concert hall, and an island.[15]

Berlioz continues this portion of his *Mémoires* with a denunciation of lowbrow beergardens in general, and of the presence of several of these desecrating "Sophie's Island." They should be relocated on "Hunter's Island" nearby, along with the clattering mills, reeking tanneries, and beergardens already established there, he declares; they ought not to be allowed to share the bower of trees surrounding the "Temple of Harmony," as he calls the Sophieninselsaal. He concludes with the opinion that "Sophie" must have had chapped hands after all.

Thus Berlioz's early impressions of persons and places in Prague. I shall say more about these, beginning with the *persons* (but excluding J.F. Kittl, whom we have already met).

Franz Škroup was the older of two musical brothers. He is best known today as the composer of the Czech national anthem, "Kde domov můj?" ("Where is my home?"), and as the first person to compose operas in the Czech language. He had been on the staff of the Ständetheater since 1823 in various capacities, becoming principal conductor in 1837. At the time of Berlioz's visit to Prague, Franz Škroup was also music director at the Old Town Synagogue.

Johann Nepomuk Škroup was, at that same time, assistant conductor to his brother Franz at the Ständetheater, musical director of the Sophienakademie, and bandmaster in a local militia corps. After having held several different musical positions in local churches, he became

---

[15] Berlioz, *Mémoires*, vol. 2, pp. 216–18. Berlioz's chaffering about Ulysses, etc. is explained by David Cairns as "a reference to Fénelon's didactic romance *Les aventures de Télémaque* (1715). Eucharis was one of Calypso's nymphs, with whom Telemachus fell in love." Hector Berlioz, trans. and ed. David Cairns, *The Memoirs of Hector Berlioz* (London: Victor Gollancz Ltd., 1969), p. 392n.

Fig. 8. Franz Škroup
Principal conductor of the Ständetheater.

Kapellmeister at the Prague Cathedral (St. Vitus) in March 1846, in the midst of the events we are encountering in our narrative.

On his first day in Prague, Berlioz also met Moritz Mildner, who was concertmaster at the Ständetheater and professor of violin at the Conservatory, where, as a young prodigy, he had received his own training as a violinist. Throughout his long career as a musician in Prague, despite vicissitudes in that city's musical life, Mildner was loved and admired; his pupils achieved fame throughout the musical world. Among the singers Berlioz met were undoubtedly some of the operatic principals of the Ständetheater, including Katharina Comet-Podhorsky, Jan Lukes, and Karl Strakaty (as their names were spelled in the German journals of the time); each sang in one or more of Berlioz's concerts in Prague. He wrote that these singers seemed to him to be artists of distinction, endowed with voices beautiful in tone and accurate in use, good all-round musicians, "like all Bohemians; and one can pay them no higher compliment."[16]

There was a kind of press conference at which Berlioz was introduced to the journalists of Prague; we may suppose that among them were F.B. Ulm ("Barnabas") and Joseph Heller ("Obolus") in their capacity as music critics, along with other Davidsbündler, since this gathering had been organized by Ambros; likewise a few other musical journalists: Rudolf Glaser, editor of *Ost und West* and *Prag*; the poet Alfred Meißner; perhaps even *Bohemia*'s Bernhard Gutt, "the redoubtable." All came expecting to meet some kind of monster. As Ambros wrote many years later:

> Johann Hoffmann, a music dealer in Prague, had in his shop a plaster reproduction of the famous bust of the Emperor Caracalla in the Capitoline Museum in Rome. When horrified customers inquired about this tigerish countenance distorted with rage, the waggish Hoffmann would say, with a straight face, "It is a portrait of the famous Berlioz." People believed this all the more readily since next to it stood a bust of Carl Maria von Weber; they found it quite in order that a

---

[16] Berlioz, *Mémoires*, vol. 2, p. 220. Berlioz frequently expresses admiration for Bohemians as musicians. Anton Reicha, a Bohemian and a colleague of Beethoven, was one of Berlioz's teachers of music in Paris. Initially resentful towards Reicha as a teacher of academic counterpoint, Berlioz came to admire him as a composer. A.W. Ambros, in his youth, studied Reicha's "Compositionslehre."

Fig. 9. From Kleinseite, a view of the Oʟᴅ and Nᴇᴡ Tᴏᴡɴs across the river
Old Town and Karlsbrücke to the left; to the right of centre is the Schützeninsel; behind it can be seen the poplars of the Sophieninsel.

composer who, in his "Marche au supplice," superimposes G minor and D-flat major without regard for the laws of figured bass and for musical decorum, should look like the Roman emperor who slew his own brother in the arms of their mother.[17]

There are other *dramatis personae* to come, of course; I have commented here upon only those few mentioned by Berlioz in his account of his introduction to people and places in Prague. We turn now to the *places*.

The "mountain" of which Berlioz writes in the Hradschin (Hradčany), which is on the left bank of the Moldau (Vltava). This hill is a respectable climb for a person in middle years, but by no means a "mountain"— hence Berlioz's persiflage about Mounts Vesuvius and Etna. Berlioz and his party crossed the river on the Karlsbrücke (or "Bridge of Prague," as it was then most often called) to the left bank of the Moldau, then puffed their way up inclines and stairways to the Hrad (the Royal Palace) and the Cathedral. From a few points along the way one can, looking upstream, indeed see "Hunter's" and "Sophie's" islands.[18]

As Sophieninsel the latter island bore the name, at the time of Berlioz's visit, of the Archduchess Sophie of Bavaria, daughter-in-law of Emperor Franz and mother of Franz Josef; it was previously known as

---

[17] A.W. Ambros, *Bunte Blätter: Skizzen und Studien für Freunde der Musik und der bildenden Kunst*, 2 vols. (Leipzig: Leuckart, 1872, 1874), vol. 1 (1872), pp. 98–99. Emingerová tells the story differently. She attributes it to Berlioz, not to Ambros, and the shopkeeper is not Hoffmann but Hoffmann's father-in-law and competitor, Marco Berra ("Berlioz à Prague," pp. 170–71). Emingerová provides no references for these assertions.

[18] The Schützeninsel, "Hunter's Island" (Střelecký ostrov) forms part of Klein Venedig ("Little Venice"), while a much larger island downstream, the Hetzeninsel (Ostrov Štvanica) was called Groß Venedig. In the sixteenth century the Schützeninsel became headquarters of the Prague Sharpshooters' Corps, a gift to the Corps from Emperor Ferdinand I, hence its name. A guidebook for visitors to Prague dated 1830 says: "Shaded paths lead to the Shooting House, in the pleasant salon of which dances are held; many tables are always set to welcome guests." On certain religious holidays there are fireworks on the island. W.A. Gerle, *Prag und seine Merkwürdigkeiten*, 2nd ed. (Prague: Borrosch, 1830), p. 20. Until 1841 the only bridge across the river was the Karlsbrücke. In that year a second bridge was completed; it crossed the river at the southern tip of the Schützeninsel, and was named Kaiser Franzens Kettenbrücke. A chain suspension bridge, as its name indicates, it was perhaps not visible to Berlioz and his companions from the Hradčany, because of its lacework structure and the haze Berlioz mentions. The present bridge on this site is the Bridge of the First of May (Most 1. Máje), named after the Workers' Festival held on the island on 1 May 1890.

Färberinsel (the reason will become apparent); in 1848 its name was changed yet again, to "Slavic Island" (Slovanský ostrov), so named after the Slavic Congress held in Prague that year. A guidebook of 1830 describes the Sophieninsel under its previous name:

> The Färberinsel is slight of circumference, wreathed by avenues of poplars. . . . Pragers come here in the mornings to drink mineral water; at midday and in the evenings they play cards and visit the hot and cold baths provided there. In recent years there has been a wooden bridge connecting the island with the New Town.
>
> Apart from the bath houses and changing huts, there is a bleaching and dyeing works on the little island, whose southern and northern tips provide delightful vistas.[19]

In that same year (1830) the island changed its character; upon it was built a so-called Resourcen-Gebäude, including a Kasino; I assume this is the Sophieninselsaal of our narrative (the word translated literally is "Sophie's Island Room"). Berlioz gave concerts there on 19 and 25 January and 7 and 17 April 1846. (The present Kasino on the island dates from 1896.)

In his letters, Berlioz refers to the Sophieninselsaal as a ballroom ("une salle de redoute"), which it was, among other things. He sent an illustration of it to his sister Nanci Pal in Grenoble. In his accompanying letter, dated Breslau 24 March and Prague 25 March 1846, he describes the island itself:

> Sophie's Island is in the middle of the Moldau, close to the town, and it must be lovely in springtime, when the leaves are opening up and the flowers are blooming.[20]

The Sophienakademie was a singing school located, not on "Sophie's Island," as Berlioz thought, but on the Liliengasse. It was founded in 1840 by Alois Jelen, a composer and state archivist. Jelen was one of the musical conservatives in Prague; he was not favourably impressed in

---

[19] Gerle, *Prag . . . Merkwürdigkeiten*, p. 20. Gerle's description of the Färberinsel (formerly "Sophieninsel") is in sharp contrast to that of Berlioz written sixteen years earlier (see p. 32). It was the dyeing works mentioned by Gerle that gave the island its later name "Färberinsel" (*Färber* means "dyer").

[20] Berlioz, *Correspondance*, vol. 3, p. 329.

Fig. 10. Looking downstream, Hradschin in the distance. Schützeninsel and Sophieninsel are in the middleground to the left of the water tower (tall structure just to the right of centre).

1846 by Berlioz's concerts there. As we have seen, J.N. Škroup was music director of the Akademie at the time of Berlioz's visit. The political upheavals of 1848 were felt even by so apparently innocuous an organization as the Sophienakademie: Škroup was forced to resign as music director.[21]

Of course, the republican and agnostic Hector Berlioz was in 1846 oblivious to most Austrian political undercurrents; hence his tactless remarks on the hilltop about the washerwoman's red face and chapped hands. Not even in private would Ambros or Hanslick have made rude comments about members of the Royal Household. Berlioz could hardly have been expected to know that the island was named after the Archduchess Sophie (whom he had met earlier in Vienna); but this would not have made the scene less embarrassing for the two Pragers.

Years later Hanslick wrote about one aspect of the political situation in Prague at just the time of Berlioz's visit there:

> It goes without saying (but nobody admits it nowadays) that in Prague, prior to 1848, all private instruction,[22] like public instruction, was given exclusively in the German language. Aristocracy and bourgeoisie, the whole cultivated middle class in Prague, spoke only German, and knew only as much Bohemian as enabled them to make themselves understood by domestic servants, labourers, and country folk. Even my mother, whose parents were from Vienna, and we brothers and sisters picked up only as much Bohemian as we needed around the house. I never learned to read and write Czech, never recited the paternoster or the multiplication table otherwise than in German. Never (and to me this is perhaps the most remarkable) could I have deciphered a Bohemian theatre playbill.
>
> The Prague Theatre [Ständetheater] was German. On Sundays only, at around 4:00 in the afternoon, three hours before the German performance was due to begin, would there be a play in Czech. One sent one's domestic servants to these Bohemian performances; none of our circle ever went to them. In my day, in Prague, it would never have occurred to anyone to challenge the precedence of the German

---

[21] "D-.", "Aus Prag: August 1849," *Neue Zeitschrift für Musik*, vol. 31, no. 20 (5 September 1849), p. 102.

[22] Hanslick refers here to his own instruction in music from Tomaschek.

language—indeed, its exclusive rights in polite society, in the arts and sciences, in the schools and the civil administration.

My father mastered written and spoken Czech perfectly; he even made German translations of songs composed by Tomaschek to Bohemian verses. But with us and his friends he always spoke German. These friends included W.A. Swoboda, a professor of the humanities and one of the most accomplished of artists in the Czech language and in translating from it.[23] From my boyhood years, I can recall other Czechs who were persons of considerable eminence: Palacký (who, as is well known, wrote his history of the Bohemian people in German so that it would be widely read);[24] Hanka, the famous "discoverer" of the *Königinhof* Manuscript;[25] the distinguished physiologist Purkinje,[26] among others. I never heard them speak anything but German with my father. Since they conversed only about learned matters, about art and politics, it was obvious that Czech would not do.

It was not until the mid-forties, shortly before my departure from the University of Vienna, that the Czech nationalistic movement made itself publicly noticeable. It was even then quite innocuous and restrained: a concert, for example, would include a Bohemian chorus or a Bohemian song by Johann Nepomuk Škroup. He was the younger brother of Franz Škroup, music director of the Ständetheater, who is renowned as the composer of one single song, "Where is my home?" J.N. Škroup, on the other hand . . . was a formidably prolific and mediocre composer. He was one of the first, who, rejected and ignored

---

[23] Wenzel Alois Swoboda (1791–1849), Czech author and political figure. Translated the *Königinhof* Manuscript into German (see note 25 below). During Eduard Hanslick's youth Swoboda was professor of humanities at the Kleinseitner Gymnasium in Prague.

[24] Franz Palacký (1798–1876), *Geschichte von Böhmen: Größentheils nach Urkunden und Handschriften* (Prague: Kronberger & Weber, 1836–67). Subsequently there were several other editions in German and Czech. Palacký was one of the most renowned historians of his day. Hanslick was not alone in noticing the irony: if this history of the Bohemian people had been published in their own language, there would have been few who could have read it.

[25] Wenzel Hanka (1791–1861) perpetrated two of the most flagrant literary hoaxes of the nineteenth century: the *Königinhof* and the *Grünberg* "Manuscripts." These did nothing to diminish his reputation as a philologist. Publisher Hoffmann in Prague brought out a song composed by Eduard Hanslik (*sic*) to verses from one of Hanka's forgeries. See Jitka Ludvová, "Zur Biographie Eduard Hanslicks," *Studien zur Musikwissenschaft: Beihefte der Denkmäler der Tonkunst in Österreich*, vol. 37 (1986), p. 44.

[26] J.E. Purkinje (1787–1869) was professor of pathology at the universities of Prague and Breslau, and author of a famous book about the central nervous system.

by the German-speaking public, began to support the newborn Czech Nationalist Party, that small but vocal minority.[27]

There is no evidence in Eduard Hanslick's own concert reviews of 1844 and 1845 to suppose that J.N. Škroup had been "rejected and ignored by the German-speaking public." Here is an excerpt from "Ed–d.'s" review of a performance in the Ständetheater of Ludwig Spohr's oratorio *The Fall of Babylon* (the performance took place on 23 December 1844):

> Prague's finest musical forces combined to make up an outstanding chorus and orchestra: the Tonkünstlergesellschaft, the Opera, the Cäcilienverein, and the Sophienakademie, with a total of three hundred musicians. To control such masses of performers is no small accomplishment; our first and warmest thanks, therefore, must go to Kapellmeister Franz Škroup, who conducted this long and difficult oratorio with the same competence and meticulousness as distinguishes all his performances of major works. Honour is due also to Messrs Škroup (the younger) and [Anton] Apt, who trained the choristers, and to Professor Mildner, who led the strings.[28]

Hector Berlioz had a good opinion of J.N. Škroup; indeed, he trusted Škroup and his Akademie to prepare the choral passages of *Romeo and Juliet* for his final concert in Prague, which was held in the Sophieninselsaal on 17 April 1846. Berlioz wrote:

> Now I must tell you about the Prague Singing Academy [the Sophienakademie]. A choral society pretty much like all the others in Germany, it is made up for the most part of amateur singers belonging to the middle class of society. The younger Monsieur Škroup is the conductor. It is a choir of about ninety singers. Most of its members are musicians, good sight-readers, and endowed with fresh and resonant voices. It is not the goal of this society to study and perform older works

---

[27] Hanslick, *Leben*, vol. 1, pp. 15–17. This is a sketch from memory. We cannot here add details or temper Hanslick's exaggerations. The sketch is presumably accurate enough for our purpose, which is to give some idea of the political climate of Prague in 1848. Of course, Czech nationalism was not the only political issue in the 1848 uprising.

[28] Eduard Hanslick [here "Ed–d."], "Der Fall Babylons: Oratorium in 2 Abtheilungen von L. Spohr," *Prag*, no. 207 (26 December 1844), pp. 836–37; no. 208 (28 December 1844), pp. 841–42. The quotation is from the second instalment, p. 842.

to the total exclusion of all contemporary productions, as is the case with many other singing academies of the same type. . . .

Its conductor is an intelligent artist, hence he admits into the Temple of Harmony[29] not only modern composers, but even living ones! Along with an oratorio by Bach or Handel he will put the choir to work on Monsieur Marx's *Moses* (Marx is an accomplished critic and theoretician very much alive in Berlin),[30] or an operatic excerpt or an anthem of a vintage much too recent to be entitled to academic consideration. For example, I recall hearing, the first time I went to one of their gatherings, a choral fantasia on Bohemian national melodies composed by Monsieur Škroup;[31] it charmed me with its originality. Never before or since have I heard such piquant vocal configurations executed with such animation, such vivid contrasts, such cohesion, precision, and beautiful tone. When I thought of those dense and ponderous compilations of chords I have too often had inflicted upon me on other such occasions, this lively piece, so exquisitely performed, had an effect on my ear something like that of the fresh and fragrant air of a forest on a beautiful summer's night upon the lungs of a prisoner just released from his fetid dungeon.

Sophie's Academy . . . presents each year a number of public performances accompanied by the orchestra of the Theatre[32] conducted by the older Škroup. These splendid renditions, prepared over a long time with care and with exemplary patience, always draw a good house, an elite audience of people for whom music is neither a diversion nor a chore, but a noble and serious passion to which they devote the full power of their intelligence, and all their sensibility, all their enthusiasm.[33]

"During his sojourn in Prague, Berlioz was our only thought, our sole preoccupation," wrote Hanslick in his account of the meeting between

---

[29] "The Temple of Harmony" is Berlioz's nickname for the Sophieninselsaal.

[30] Adolf Bernhard Marx's oratorio *Moses* was performed in Prague on 6 April 1864. Berlioz was in Prague at the time but I do not know whether he attended this performance. *Moses* was coldly received by the music critics in Prague. Bernhard Gutt reviewed the performance and wrote on *Moses* for *Bohemia*; we discuss these two articles in our concluding chapter.

[31] Presumably "Děvy krásné, děvy naše" by J.N. Škroup, "a nosegay of patriotic tunes." Emingerová ("Berlioz à Prague," p. 173) says that the occasion was a concert on 16 January 1846 by the Sophienakademie; from Berlioz's own account, however, it is evident that it was not a public performance but a rehearsal. Berlioz recruited the alto soloist for his *Romeo and Juliet* at this rehearsal. See p. 93, note 2 below.

[32] I.e., the Ständetheater.

[33] Berlioz, *Mémoires*, vol. 2, pp. 237–38.

Hector Berlioz and Wenzel Johann Tomaschek, who had been Hanslick's own teacher of music. I quote from this account in a moment, but first I must provide some background.

Tomaschek was a gigantic figure in Prague's musical life, renowned as composer and teacher, but not formally connected with the Conservatory or with any other musical institution. His residence was an eighteenth-century mansion built upon Gothic foundations and with Renaissance vaulting; it survives, and is known as Palais Tomaschek (Tomáškův palác). Currently it is being restored. Recalling his four years as a pupil of Tomaschek, Hanslick wrote:

> Tomaschek gave his lessons exclusively at his home, which was way up in the Kleinseite, facing the Palais Waldstein [Valdštejnský palác]. From the Roßmarkt [now Wenceslas Square, Václavské náměstí] it was a good half hour's walk, over the stone bridge [Karlsbrücke], not very enticing at some ungodly hour in the dead of winter.[34]

So it was across the river and some distance up the hill that Berlioz went to see Tomaschek, with young Hanslick as his guide. Berlioz may not have been as insouciant as he seems in Hanslick's description of this meeting; every performing artist who came to Prague was expected to pay respects to Tomaschek without delay. It was understood that a musician's success with audiences in Prague would be in no small measure dependent upon Tomaschek's favourable impression.[35] Here is Hanslick's description of this momentous encounter.

> I can see myself with Berlioz as if were only yesterday, tramping over the Moldau Bridge,[36] beyond which lived Himself, Herr General Bass.[37]

---

[34] Hanslick, *Leben*, vol. 1, p. 29.

[35] Alexander Buchner, trans. Roberta Finlayson Samsour, *Franz Liszt in Bohemia* (London: Peter Nevill, 1962), p. 43.

[36] It seems unlikely that Ritter Berlioz would have arrived on foot at the Palace of Tomaschek, the Musical Pontiff of Prague. Perhaps he and his young interpreter went by diligence (i.e., a horse-drawn conveyance).

[37] *Generalbass*, in English "figured bass," is given as "General Bass" by Hanslick to show a good-natured contempt for the worst excesses of academic harmony and counterpoint. See Hanslick's remarks about Fétis in "Ritter Berlioz in Prague." In Hanslick's writings, Tomaschek is variously referred to as "the Dalai Lama of Music in Prague," as "the Pontiff," "the Grand Old Man," and similar terms in which are mixed admiration and exasperation.

Fig. 11. Crossing the Moldau on the way to the "Contrapuntal Residence"
the KARLSBRÜCKE, viewed from the Old Town.

Fig. 12. WENZEL JOHANN TOMASCHEK
"Herr General Bass."

Berlioz had attached himself firmly to me; I was so overwhelmed by this honour that I was in dread of meeting somebody I knew.

A few steps before we got to the Contrapuntal Residence, Berlioz revealed to me, with engaging nonchalance, that he had never heard of Tomaschek, and even less did he know a note of this composer's music. So now, in a hastily condensed version, I had to supply my foreigner with his missing chapter of the history of music under the title "Tomaschek." In order not to get Berlioz muddled with a list of Tomaschek's many works, I boiled it down for him, with considerable emphasis, to one title, a *Requiem* by which Tomaschek set great store, and in fact a very fine composition of his. We entered, and there ensued a scene, partly funny and partly painful, of the kind known as "interpreting." It was a piecemeal dragging back and forth of trivial sentences, yet often difficult to render. The embarrassment between the arch-conservative and the revolutionary artist made it all not very rewarding. Fortunately, Berlioz did not forget his magic word: right on cue he said how gratified he was at meeting personally the composer of "that magnificent *Requiem*." The old man, somewhat gruff from having lived so much alone, accepted this homage with a slight nod and the announcement that he would like to go to Berlioz's forthcoming concert. Such an odd and perfunctory encounter would have been unlikely to provide the slightest glimpse of Tomaschek's artistic nature.[38]

So the two visitors departed, having left two tickets to the concert on Tomaschek's piano, as was the custom. Hanslick concludes his version of the story:

Afterwards, upon reflection, Berlioz's only comment on his new acquaintance was: "He seems infatuated with himself."[39]

Among the musical functionaries Berlioz met during his first few days in Prague were, presumably, the managers of the two halls in which he was to perform, the Sophieninselsaal and the Ständetheater. As will become apparent, Berlioz's account in his *Mémoires* is particularly unreliable where it mentions these two halls and their managers. From

---

[38] Hanslick, *Leben*, vol. 1, pp. 58–59.
[39] Ibid., vol. 1, p. 59.

Berlioz's journals, however, it is possible to construct a schedule of his concerts in Prague, as follows:

1. 19 January (Monday)   Sophieninselsaal
2. 25 January (Sunday)   Sophieninselsaal
3. 27 January (Tuesday) Ständetheater
4. 31 March   (Tuesday) Ständetheater
5. 7 April   (Tuesday) Sophieninselsaal
6. 17 April   (Friday)   Sophieninselsaal

Berlioz wrote:

> The theatre, when I saw it (in 1845), seemed to me a dark, poky, and grubby place with a very bad sound. I am informed that it has been renovated since then, and that the new director, Monsieur Hoffmann, is making commendable efforts to bring it back to its former prosperity; it had been allowed to run down under the previous administration.[40]

Berlioz is here speaking of the Ständetheater; I point this out because in a moment he will speak of the Sophieninselsaal as "the theatre." The year 1845 in the above quotation is obviously an error: it should read "1846."[41]

The new director of the Ständetheater was Johann H. Hoffmann (1802–1865), a Viennese. According to Wurzbach,[42] Hoffmann was awarded the appointment on 13 August 1845, and took up his duties at around Easter of 1846 (Easter fell on 12 April). By that date Berlioz had already conducted his two concerts at the Ständetheater (see the schedule above); his two remaining concerts in Prague were held in the Sophieninselsaal. So it seems that Berlioz had to deal with Hoffmann's predecessor, Johann August Stöger (1791–1861), another Austrian (he was born in Stockerau). Of Stöger, Berlioz wrote:

---

[40] Berlioz, *Mémoires*, vol. 2, p. 220.
[41] Berlioz wrote this account in 1847 or early 1848. Katinka Emingerová, in her essay "Hector Berlioz à Prague," p. 168, says that Berlioz visited Prague briefly in 1844, but provides no evidence in support of this questionable assertion.
[42] Wurzbach, *Biographisches Lexikon*, vol. 9, p. 172. I give this, instead of an "s.v." citation, for the reason that Wurzbach provides biographies of no fewer than ten Hoffmanns with the first name "Johann." As I say in my text at several points, there is confusion.

> He was an honourable man, not very experienced in musical matters, just like all theatre directors, but, unlike the others, beloved and esteemed by his staff, who showed their regrets very fervently when, under pressure of his private business ventures, he had to relinquish the directorship.[43]

Far from being "not very experienced in musical matters," Stöger began his career as an opera singer; he possessed a ravishing tenor voice, but was small of stature and clumsy in motion, so he was unconvincing on the stage. It was he who appointed Moritz Mildner as concertmaster and Franz Škroup as principal conductor; it was he who brought the Prague Opera into the ranks of the foremost in Europe. His private business ventures included another theatre in Prague (it was not a success financially), and a large brickworks out of town. Stöger formally relinquished command in the twelfth year of his directorship at around Easter 1846, as mentioned above, and was given a magnificent and affectionate sendoff by his staff; it included a torchlight parade with music. He subsequently became director of the Josefstädtertheater in Vienna, but within less than a decade he was back at his old job in the Ständetheater in Prague.

To add to our confusion, during the previous November (1845) the journals in Prague reported that Hoffmann had made a vigorous beginning in his new appointment as director of the Ständetheater. Presumably there was an overlap: Hoffmann started out in an acting capacity and did not assume the official title of Director until Stöger's contract expired the following April; so it would seem that Johann H. Hoffmann was in charge of the day-to-day operations of the theatre until then.

More confusion: Berlioz, in a letter dated Prague 21 January 1846, two days after his first concert there and six days before his first (of two) concerts in the Ständetheater, enthusiastically describes his reception by the music lovers of the city. He continues:

> There's only one fly in the ointment, an insect of whom I wish in vain to rid myself, and who bites as much as he can out of me. I refer to the director of the theatre. His position entitles him to twelve per cent of

---

[43] Berlioz, *Mémoires*, vol. 2, pp. 222–23.

Fig. 13. The Ständetheater

the gross receipts at concerts there; and when the receipts are considerable, as they were last Monday, that's a crushing tithe. So, what can I
do? Just the usual: render unto Caesar that which is not Caesar's.[44]

Was the insect Stöger or Hoffmann?

The concert "last Monday" was held, not in "the theatre" (the
Ständetheater was familiarly known simply as "das Theater"), but in the
Sophieninselsaal, as noted above. Of the administrative arrangements
of the latter I know nothing. I doubt, however, that its manager rejoiced
in so grand a title as "Direktor." So Berlioz is complaining here about his
arrangements with the director of the Ständetheater; whether the
twelve per cent perquisite went to Stöger or to Hoffmann we shall
perhaps never know. As Oskar Schürer says, their change of command
took place at a turbulent time.[45]

Not surprisingly, there is another Johann Hoffmann; we have already
met him in passing. He is the music dealer in Prague who had, in his
shop window, a plaster bust of the bland and refined head of Carl Maria
von Weber (who, incidentally, was himself once music director at the
Ständetheater) alongside that of the Emperor Caracalla in his role as
"the famous Berlioz." This Johann Hoffmann is, of course, easily
confused with Director Hoffmann; in his letters, Berlioz occasionally
mentions a Hoffmann, but does not identify him clearly.

Johann Hoffmann was more than a retailer of music; his shop on
what is now the Malá Karlova was part of a little empire that included
piano sales and service, a music lending library, and a music publishing
business. As music publisher, Hoffmann is remembered in Czechoslova-
kia for his encouragement of Czech composers, including Kittl,
Tomaschek, and the brothers Škroup. He was one of Prague's most
enthusiastic devotees and promoters of new music, which makes him a
stronger candidate that Director Hoffmann for Berlioz's friendship.

Hanslick wrote:

> I toiled industriously at the keyboard to make myself acquainted with
> the new music; in this I was greatly assisted by the excellent sheet-
> music establishment owned by J. Hoffmann. Hoffmann's was distin-

[44] Berlioz, *Correspondance*, vol. 3, p. 308.
[45] Oscar Schürer, *Prag: Kultur, Kunst, Geschichte*, 5th ed. (Munich: Callwey; Brünn: Rohrer, 1935), p. 306.

guished, not only for its great variety of offerings, but also (and more importantly) for the fact that it published a comprehensive printed catalogue. I have never found such a catalogue in any Viennese music shop; yet this is the only means by which a person seriously interested in music, and not involved in it merely for entertainment, can systematically gather information about the whole terrain. Every newly published composition was promptly acquired and listed by Hoffmann's lending library; and there, being a subscriber, I replenished my musical fodder almost daily. Hence, I was the butt of many witticisms about the fact that I was never seen on the streets of Prague without my music case under my arm.[46]

From his arrival in Prague on 14 January to his first concert on the 19th, Berlioz and his new friends were busy. They assembled an orchestra: the twenty-five resident musicians of the Ständetheater were augmented by a contingent of professors and senior pupils from the Conservatory, a few amateurs, and some bandsmen from the local garrison, the total being eighty-two players—a huge orchestra by the standards of the time. Rehearsals must have been long and arduous, but exciting; Berlioz arrived at them accompanied by his "guard of honour," as one violinist called it: Ambros and Kittl (and, we may suppose, the young student Hanslick modestly walking at a respectful interval behind them). Kittl brought his students so they could learn by Berlioz's example how an orchestral rehearsal ought to be conducted (although somebody noticed that Berlioz did not provide his players with cues for their entries). A few days after his first concert, Berlioz wrote in a letter to a friend in Paris:

> I arrived here expecting to find myself amongst old-fashioned pedants who would hear of nothing but Mozart, who stood ready to boo every modern composer. Instead I have found artists who are dedicated, attentive, of exceptional intelligence, ready to rehearse four hours without a murmur of complaint, and more enthusiastic over my music

---

[46] Hanslick, *Leben*, vol. 1, p. 40.

at the end of the second rehearsal than I could ever have dared to hope.[47]

Hector Berlioz had, in the extravagant language with which some writers like to describe the events of our narrative, "smashed the gates of Prague."[48] Then came the great day, Monday 19 January 1846.

> The hour of battle approached. Everybody who counted for anything in Prague, by virtue of culture, wealth, or rank, converged upon the Sophieninselsaal. The aristocracy was represented by all the great names: Lobkowitz, Thun, Nostitz, Schlick, who were doing their duty as patrons of the arts, and who set the tone. Celebrities of the artistic world, ladies of the foremost families of the bourgeoisie, music lovers, intellectuals, journalists, students—whether out of interest or out of curiosity, everybody came.[49]

No doubt the Davidsbündler were there to witness their vindication, including "Renatus," his head buzzing with new and powerful impressions from his daily contact with Berlioz, listening to the famous composer's views on music and life, communicating the Master's instructions to the orchestral musicians, becoming acquainted with the compositions from the composer's own viewpoint. Can it be doubted that those January days in 1846 had a profound effect upon Eduard Hanslick's whole career as music critic?

His review of the concert follows.

---

[47] Berlioz, *Correspondance*, vol. 3, p. 309. For a more detailed account of the makeup of Berlioz's orchestra in Prague, see August Wilhelm Ambros, "Zweites Sendschreiben an die Musikfreunde Prags," *Prager Zeitung*, no. 13 (22 January 1846), p. 161.
[48] Emingerová, "Berlioz à Prague," p. 171.
[49] Ibid., p. 173.

IV

Hanslick's Essay "Ritter Berlioz in Prague"

No, they cannot touch me for coining. I am the king himself.
— King Lear[1]

I HAVE JUST COME from the first of the Berlioz concerts and I   5
have to say at the outset that Berlioz is the sublimest
manifestation in the realm of musical poetry since Beethoven. This
opinion is the inescapable result of impressions I have just had and
of my study of his works and reflection upon them. From me you
will have no timid "on the one hand . . . but on the other," no   10
judicious turning of phrase. Berlioz has divided the music critics
into factions: whether we like it or not, we have to choose between
the Guelphs and the Ghibellines. I have taken my stand, and I
reiterate it gladly and without reservation: this man, who was at first
ignored, then ridiculed, then reviled and persecuted, is a powerful   15
intellect and a great poet in musical sounds.

No, kind reader, that was not dashed off in the heat of the
moment. Whatever their faults, my music reviews cannot be
accused of effusiveness, and this one is no exception. For some years
I have been acquainted with such of Berlioz's compositions as have   20
been available for study, and have heard several times the works
performed here on the 19th of this month. My admiration and
understanding increased with each hearing. I would like to try to
support my opinion by enumerating the most significant of the
objections raised against his compositions, and, as far as possible,   25
by refuting them.

The main accusation (and most of the lesser ones can be sub-
sumed under it) goes like this: in the first place, Berlioz's works do

---

Translation of Eduard Hanslick [here "Eduard Hanslik"], "Ritter Berlioz in Prag," *Ost und West*, vol. 10, no. 9 (22 January 1846), pp. 35–36; no. 10 (24 January 1846), pp. 38–40.

[1] William Shakespeare, *King Lear*, IV, vi.

not appeal to the general public; in the second place, his works are rejected by the critics. How can this be if, as you claim, they are full of poetry and intellectual content?

Concerning the first point, I am bound to reply, with some regret, that the opinion of the general public is no longer a criterion for assessing the merit of a musical artwork. There are two reasons for this. The first is that scientific investigation of music, whether on the level of theory or that of practical music-making, is being more and more superficially pursued. The second is that in recent times there has been an increasing divergence between public taste on the one hand and the Ideal of true art on the other. We no longer take it for granted that all music is for everyone and everyone is for all music. It takes knowledge, and it takes prolonged familiarity with music, to understand a composition that is in any way complicated in form and content. Anyone who is not at home in the musical repertoire will, upon hearing something new and different, stumble over awkward corners, and will be put off when confronted by unfamiliar musical configurations. The great majority are not in a position to comprehend a musical work of generous dimensions and predominantly intellectual content; and without comprehension there can be no pleasure. The best possible artwork is one in which *both* aspects of the beautiful are united, namely the intellectually and the sensuously stimulating, to the satisfaction of experts and laymen alike. Certainly this ideal is not unachievable. But it seems that in our time artists have to incline towards the one or the other. I would be foolish to blame the general public for the fact that it prefers *La Somnambula*[2] to *St. Paul*;[3] this preference is an inevitable consequence of the nature of music itself, and of music's relation to aesthetical cultivation in general. I would not for the life of me insist that the majority of people are invariably delighted by inferior music; but I do insist that a certain category of the musically

---

[2] Opera by Bellini.
[3] Oratorio by Mendelssohn. In an earlier review, Hanslick compares it with Lessing's *Nathan der Weise* and says that it is the greatest of Mendelssohn's compositions. Eduard Hanslick [here "Ed–d."], "Erstes Konzert des Konservatoriums am 23. Februar," *Prag*, no. 32 (24 February 1845), p. 127.

beautiful (and only the very grandest of musical endeavours belong
to it) remains to them forever inaccessible.

In this regard, the visual arts are much better off; unlike music
they represent the visible, the given, the actual; and the actual is
comprehensible. On the other hand, poetry, in its most exalted   5
kinds, has in common with music the characteristic of esotericism;
but it has the advantage over music that it possesses a much wider
circle of initiates, and is therefore less exclusive in its effectiveness.
Who would dare to dismiss Klopstock, Jean Paul, Hölderlin, or
Immermann, just because they never achieved popularity and   10
never had any effect upon the masses? Beethoven fared badly in this
regard, and to some extent still does; but would anyone take away
from him the garland of immortality just because he never appealed
to the great public? This, dear reader, is also the legitimate question
when we come to Berlioz; and it is perhaps well enough answered by   15
what I have just said.

But what about the critics, those experts *ex officio*, those infallible
oracles: how is it that they also reject Berlioz?

The reason lies in the novelty of the phenomenon. Disdaining
the well-trodden, Berlioz's genius has opened up new avenues. The   20
musical formations that he conjures up have run ahead of theory,
and this is what he is accused of. He does not write in the Mozartian
style, or in Spohrian, or even in Beethovenian: he writes in the
Berliozian style, and that is what people find puzzling. The old
familiar standards of criticism are inadequate for new creations, and   25
that vexes us. Nowadays we have reviewers in the journals (there are
a few honourable exceptions) for whom the rules of art are axi-
omatic and valid for all time; anything that refuses to conform to
this standard is pronounced defective. They have not comprehended
Berlioz, therefore Berlioz is incomprehensible; he has not pandered   30
to their taste, therefore he has no taste. This is the way these gentry
brush him aside; and the more cleverly they do it, the worse it is for
the Cause. However, a few men have taken sides with Berlioz, have
gallantly taken their places at the barricades, and have contended
with might and main for the Apostle of Genius and Poetry. But take   35
note that these were all men who were well acquainted with

Berlioz's compositions. They studied before they judged; they examined before they spoke. Not until then did they shout Berlioz's name enthusiastically and pay homage to the new King.

First and foremost there was Robert Schumann in Leipzig;[4] then
5   Professor Griepenkerl in Brunswick;[5] then Becher in Vienna[6] and August Wilhelm Ambros in Prague.[7] I associate myself proudly with these men. I am far from being their equal in knowledge and experience, yet I do not fall short of them in enthusiasm for beauty and in love of truth. I have never considered my name so important
10   that I have inflicted it upon the readers of my reviews; but today it appears in print, herewith, for the first time. In partisan matters a man has to put his whole person on the line; and, where a noble cause is at stake, anonymity is for the hangman.

Let us consider now the main accusations brought by the critics
15   against Berlioz's compositions. To begin with, irregularity and arbitrariness of form. It is true that Berlioz does not confine himself to the old forms, and tramples all over their ruins boldly and without restraint, as has happened in the past. But the laws of form, insofar as they result from the eternal conditions of beauty, he has
20   neither violated nor subverted; he has merely extended them and liberated them from the shackles of convention. This emancipation did not come out of the blue and from revolutionary insolence; it was done in the service of the Idea. A gigantic mind requires a gigantic body. "Onward!" is the battle cry of all spiritual endeavour.
25   Who would take it upon himself to condemn music alone among the arts to the curse of stagnation? Particularly since with Beethoven the Romantic principle took on life and validity in music, the possibility, nay the necessity of evolving ever further has become

---

[4] Schumann, "Aus dem Leben eines Künstlers." For the full citation see Bibliography.
[5] Griepenkerl, *Ritter Berlioz in Braunschweig.*
[6] Becher, "Über Hektor Berlioz." For the full citation see Bibliography. Alfred Julius Becher (1803–1848), composer and influential music critic in Vienna, was executed for high treason following the suppression of the November uprising in Vienna in 1848.
[7] August Wilhelm Ambros [here "Jur. Dr. August Wilhelm Ambros aus Prag"], "Die Ouverture zu Shakespeare's 'König Lear' von Hektor Berlioz," *Wiener Allgemeine Musik-Zeitung,* beginning vol. 5, no. 120 (7 October 1845), p. 477. For the full citation see Bibliography.

fully potentialized. For the essence of Romanticism consists in just this: that in its external manifestations the Idea no longer limits itself, is no longer satisfied with itself as in Classicism, but by means of its infinitude bursts through form and soars into the realm of the immeasurable. Yet Berlioz transcends Beethoven no more than   5
Beethoven transcends Mozart. You acknowledge Beethoven's turbulent genius with praise; would you close the door behind him?[8]

The second accusation is lack of melody. But what do you mean by "melody"? Are the themes from the "Pilgrims' March" and the *Roman Carnival* not melodies? The motives of the *Lear* and *Waverley*   10
Overtures? That pallid, wonderful theme of the *Symphonie fantastique*? Of course you cannot expect Berlioz to be always chasing after new themes, nor indeed (as Robert Schumann cautioned us) after those Italian melodies which everyone knows by heart before they have even begun.[9] Berlioz's themes have some-   15
thing astringent about them, something out of the ordinary; but they are noble, pure, of the loftiest spiritual expression. Yet they do not always stand out as clearly and definitely as, for example, the "Ball" theme; frequently they are entwined and covered over with whimsical arabesques and figures. Berlioz disdains to post in front   20
of every theme a diminished seventh chord, or the dominant cadence with fermate as a guard of honour; or to dispatch a few staccato or arpeggiated triads two beats ahead as outriders.

The third and weightiest accusation is that Berlioz's musical ideas are confused and incomprehensible, and lack organic coherence.   25
His audacious flight of ideas is indeed not easily followed; and on first hearing even the best of musicians feel uneasy with it.

This brings us to the main point at issue. The critic ought not to pronounce a verdict against an artwork of massive dimensions and conception on the basis of a single hearing. Only the layman has the   30
right to attend every concert with no preparation in advance, and to announce his immediate impression according to the plumbline of

[8] The first instalment of Hanslick's "Ritter Berlioz in Prague" ends here.
[9] Robert Schumann, trans. Edward T. Cone, "A Symphony by Berlioz," in Cone, *Hector Berlioz Fantastic Symphony*, p. 241.

his own private judgement. But the position of the reviewer for
publication is a responsible one; he must *examine* the work before
passing judgement on it. I beseech you, study Berlioz's scores, and
you will see that there is in them, along with all the spontaneity, an
5   admirable intellectual coherence; and, along with all the passion, a
solid, orderly design at the core. Study his scores and you will grasp
and admire the powerful conceptions of the Master; and, when the
large-scale contours of the whole become clear to you, you will
easily discover the coherence of the smallest periods. Along with
10   score-study, or, indeed, in the absence of it, diligent attendance at
rehearsals is mandatory if you are to understand Berlioz's works
fully.*

If all the good souls who exhaled fire and smoke at the mere
thought of Berlioz had taken the trouble to become more closely
15   acquainted with the works they have castigated, many ill-consid-
ered and censorious words would not have found their way into
print. We would have been spared last year the words of the
redoubtable B. Gutt to the effect that the Overture to *King Lear* is not music.

Regarding this last point, namely the incoherence and *bizarrerie*
20   of Berlioz's ideas, this has unfortunately also been sometimes
greatly exaggerated even by his advocates. In their zeal, these
worthies often proved that twice two is not only four but also five.
Berlioz is, indeed, often obscure and peculiar in his themes, capri-
cious in the rhythmic arrangement of periods; here and there one
25   recoils at forced harmonies and abrupt modulations. It would be
absurd to deny the existence of these defects. But do they not vanish
in the dazzling aurora of his vast intellect? Do they not fade away in
the tropical glow of his imagination, the most powerful ever to have

---

* Here is the place to warn against Berlioz's *bête noire*, the piano transcription. At best a
transcription of one of his works can be no more than a tenuous guideline which makes
it somewhat easier to apprehend the work while listening to it, or to understand it once
heard. But even the best keyboard version cannot give us any idea of the effect of a
Berliozian composition, since its noblest poetry often resides in the instrumentation itself.
This is why I consider Liszt's piano arrangement of the *Symphonie fantastique*, despite
Schumann's commendation, to be quite unacceptable. With all the effort that went into
the making of it, it fails in principle. Berlioz's *Symphonie fantastique* can no more be ar-
ranged for two hands than Beethoven's Symphony in C minor [the Fifth] for two flutes.
[Hanslick's note.]

manifest itself in tones? Beethoven himself in his later works is full
of the strangest whimsicalities and eccentricities; is he any the less
for all that?

These defects of loosejointedness and *bizarrerie*, these reckless
stoppings and startings in Berlioz's compositions, are so essential a   *5*
part of the composer's personality that without them he would be
someone else. Berlioz is an individualist, not someone who walks in
the steps of another; he is an original, not a copy. Of course, there
are many people whose main concern is that the trees should not
grow up into the heavens, who say that with regard to the emotions   *10*
a composer must always conduct himself in a refined and gentle-
manly fashion, always conversing nicely, clearly and reasonably,
never giving offence to decent folk. The new musical giant is no
threat to these people, for they still have their Proch and their
Czerny and many other gentlemen who are lucid and straightfor-   *15*
ward. The enemies of Berlioz point to Mozart, who created the most
poetical works without ever becoming obscure or bizarre. But
Mozart's muse was Grace, the goddess of serenity and formal
beauty. In her service he was always able to be lucid and serene,
always intelligible and pleasing. Berlioz's muse, however, is Passion.   *20*
She does not wander happily through green meadows and fragrant
gardens singing tra-la, tra-la, but plunges out into the stormy night,
through brambles and thickets, over rocks and chasms. You know
very well that Despair does not go about in evening dress and kid
gloves; would you scold the poet for ruffling his hair and gesticulat-   *25*
ing wildly in the grip of his anguish? Berlioz has opened up to you
a fairyland Peru, rich in gold, and has told you to help yourselves,
and all you want to do is grumble and quarrel with him because here
and there in his gold mines you have found a defective nugget, and
you want to throw it at him. But make no mistake about it: your   *30*
accusations bounce off him, and there he stands, no less magnificent, now and for all time! No, you cannot touch him for coining;
he is the King himself.

Berlioz opened the concert with his *Roman Carnival* Overture, the themes of which are taken from his opera *Benvenuto Cellini*. Following some vigorously descending violin passages there emerges a simple, very appealing andante in 3/4 time, at first delicately and
5   plainly on the oboe, and then with increasingly bright and vivid coloration, until it is taken up by the full orchestra and picked out rhythmically by snare drums, cymbals, and tympani, and stands revealed in all its glory. Then, following a slight diminuendo, the allegro vivace (marked pianissimo) joins in. The scene becomes
10   more animated. Enter a masked figure; over there is another one, a third, a fourth, a whole dozen of them! Now it becomes even brisker, more active and lively until the energetic main theme bursts forth jubilantly. What a merry bustle, what deliciously Mediterranean goings-on! Always *original* and never overdone, al-
15   ways bubbling and never coarse! The overture exceeds the most far-fetched expectations regarding the famous Berliozian orchestration, and demonstrates brilliantly that in *this* art no living composer comes anywhere close to our visitor from France. For the first time we saw how many treasures lie untouched among the capabili-
20   ties of particular musical instruments, and in the handling of them in various combinations, treasures which until now every composer has lacked the magic formula, or the courage, to bring to the light of day. Many of these marvelous effects are so obvious that one wonders why they never occurred to anyone else before now: for
25   example, the piping up and down the chromatic scale by two flutes at the end of the andante, after which comes that wonderful interval of a third where the clarinet comes to rest below the waldhorn,[10] and many others. The *Roman Carnival* is among the most accessible of Berlioz's orchestral compositions, and is of such
30   overwhelming effect that the whole audience was noticeably ex-alted and excited. There may have been a few disappointed young ladies who expected that the *Roman Carnival* would be a companion piece to the *Venetian Carnival*. Mesdemoiselles, for such fiddle-faddle

---

[10]Mm. 75–80 in the Eulenburg pocket score. The "two flutes" are here flute and piccolo; the "waldhorn" is a cor anglais. From his *Mémoires* we know that Berlioz had to make substitutions for various instruments while on tour.

Berlioz is not sufficiently jocular, nor, for that matter, sufficiently serious.

There followed two songs by Berlioz with orchestral accompaniment: a ballad "Le chasseur danois" (sung by our Strakaty with vigour and enthusiasm), and "Bolero," which Madame Podhorsky rendered very brilliantly. The ballad is forthright and gripping, a breath of air from the northern forests; "Bolero" is infinitely tender and charming. With these two shorter pieces Berlioz showed that he is also capable of accommodating his titanic energy to words provided him, and of working within narrow restrictions, his spirit and impetus undiminished.

In the "Pilgrims' March" from the *Harold* Symphony is presented pictorial-literary music at its most refined. I know nothing to compare with it in the entire musical literature. The pious song of the pilgrims sounds in the distance and a faint horn call is occasionally heard, magical in its effect. Nearer and nearer this devout procession comes, slowly over the mountains. A viola adorns the evening hymn with ravishing arpeggios, and a melodious sound of tiny bells breaks in, marvelously simulated on the harp by alternate plucking of C and the B a seventh above it. The pilgrims pass by us singing; fainter and fainter becomes the song, until at last it fades away completely and only the little bell sounds.

Concluding the program was an early work of Berlioz, the famous *Symphonie fantastique*. It is the direct inspiration of the most boundless, all-consuming passion for a female beloved, a passion which throws all his thinking and feeling into a turmoil. The symphony has been criticized, and not unjustly, for being unclear and confused in parts, and less symmetrical than Berlioz's later works. But whence comes peace of mind in the terrible first awakening of Love; whence comes clarity of thought when all one can think of and feel is You, only *You* God help me, nothing but YOU!! Surely this is not merely a fictitious agony; it is an agony that has been lived through that Berlioz portrays. The *Symphonie fantastique* is the apotheosis of passion; Berlioz has written it in his life's blood. That is why this work cannot be understood merely with regard to its form; it demands *sympathy*. In my view, cold and

detached study will not serve in this instance. One must enter into the young man's passion with a full and glowing heart; one must grasp what a deep and hopeless love is like. I am not insisting that everyone who listens to the piece should first go mad with love,
5   although there would be no harm done if once in his life the listener had gone some distance in that direction. At the very least he should understand that it is *possible* to go mad with love.

Professor F[étis] in Brussels certainly never had an inkling of that sort of thing, otherwise he would not have bestowed upon the
10 young composer so abominable a letter of safe conduct into the world. The good professor, whose merits as theorist and teacher I do not wish to disparage, has taken the *Symphonie fantastique* to task (apparently after having refreshed himself with a dash of Fux and Mattheson and having sketched an invertible counterpoint for his
15 *Requiem*), and written a philippic against it. This greatly pleased the whole Armada of classicists, antichromaticists, and devotees of the figured-bass approach to musical composition. But some people were angered by it. Dear Professor, there was only one place in your critique that pleased me, and that is where you said that upon
20 hearing the *Symphonie fantastique* you had a nightmare. This is no small compliment to Berlioz's genius. No doubt he much regretted not being able to return it; for, as everyone knows, F[étis]'s compositions induce in their hearers a much calmer, more peaceful state.

25   Berlioz arranged to have narrative descriptions of his symphony handed out to the audience. These, at any rate, help to give the audience a more accurate idea of the work; yet one ought to be on guard against aesthetically misusing this form as assistance.*

The first movement, "Rêveries, Passions," is perhaps the most
30 passionate, but, from the end of the incomparable C minor introduction, the most difficult to comprehend. The crowding, flowing masses of sound confuse us at the first hearing, and only the pale, aristocratic "idée fixe" theme, which the composer aptly describes

---

* The concert program erroneously gives 1820 as the year of the first performance of the symphony. It occurred in 1830. [Hanslick's note.]

as "un certain caractère passionée, mais noble et timide," shines
forth distinctly; it seems to wander through this vast tone-painting
like that princess in the fairy tale: "Night in front of me, night
behind me." But upon closer acquaintance the sequence of ideas
becomes entirely comprehensible, and we admire the truth and   5
beauty of the movement. How yearning those reveries, how exalted
this passion! Believe me, *Fétis*, these are no "songes-creux"![11] Even
though the second movement, "Un bal," begins in 3/8 time, it is still
sombre with some enchantingly melancholy preludizing on the
two harps. But immediately the violins come in with the spirited   10
waltz theme, which is developed in three different harmonizations
and in the most interesting transformations and modulations; the
cellos have it in the concluding stretto with immense effectiveness.
The third movement, "Scène aux champs," is the most poetical in
its intentions, and is of infinite truth. Of unforgettable beauty is the   15
way the dialogue between the two shawms brings consolation to
the broken heart of the poet; the failure of the reply to appear
enables him once more to feel his solitude. What, then, is one to say
to the critics of a certain great city who explain Berlioz's compositions away as mere products of calculation and cold reflection? The   20
shawm parts, with their calling out and replying, are written for cor
anglais and oboe in the original score; Heinrich Panofka in his
report from Paris mistakenly refers to a clarinet.[12] But in our performance the first of these two parts had to be assigned to an oboe,
which produced a good effect in the lowest register. The fourth   25
movement, "Marche au supplice," is the most touching of all. How
admirable is that passage where the bassoons carry the basso
continuo in grisly staccato while the violins play the frightful
march theme above them in pizzicato; the music crumples and
suddenly the whole brass section bursts forth with shocking   30
splendour in the key of B-flat major.[13] And finally, one more time,
the pallid, consumptive image of the Beloved, cut off in the midst

---

[11] "Empty daydreams." François-Joseph Fétis, trans. Edward T. Cone, "Critical Analysis,"
in Cone, *Berlioz Fantastic Symphony*, p. 219.
[12] Heinrich Panofka, "Aus Paris," *Neue Zeitschrift für Musik*, no. 18 (3 March 1835), p. 71.
[13] Mm. 49–62 in the Eulenburg pocket score.

the falling blade.[14] Anyone who is not thrilled in his innermost depths by these notes is impervious to every kind of music. The *Symphonie fantastique* has yet a fifth movement, "Songe d'une nuit du Sabbat." The nightmare does not come to an end with the *coup*
5 *fatal*: the poet has a vision of himself surrounded by witches, demons and hideous grotesques, who celebrate their Sabbath. The witches begin their dance (a fugato in 6/8 time, full of effects),[15] in which are mixed solemn bell tones and the ponderous notes of the "Dies irae." Even here the image of the Beloved comes to him, that
10 "idée fixe," but contorted and obscene, coarsely tootled on an E-flat clarinet.[16] This movement is the cry of anguish of an overwrought imagination; it presses hard against the limits of the aesthetical. In our concert the composer was judicious and sensitive enough to omit it.
15   The kind reader will excuse me for not providing a detailed analysis of the *Symphonie fantastique*. The body is too beautiful for me to slice it up. And anyway, the great Robert Schumann (ten years ago, think of it!) has written an analysis of this work that puts every subsequent attempt into the shade.
20   Perhaps I will undertake one day a detailed critique of the other compositions of Berlioz for a musical journal.
     In conclusion I should mention the remarkable performances, which deserve highest praise. The orchestra consisted of artists some of whom received their musical training under the guidance
25 of Director J.F. Kittl, others rehearsed under Kapellmeister F. Škroup; the conducting of the famous composer in person, and the orchestra's enthusiasm for his music, did the rest.
     Even more to the credit of our city than these performances is the reception that has been accorded to Berlioz here. The total absorp-
30 tion and stillness during the playing, and the enraptured applause, were all the evidence needed to prove that the musical reputation of the people of Prague has not yet become a mere cliché. Pragers! You

---

[14] Mm. 164–69 in the Eulenburg pocket score.
[15] Beginning at m. 241 in the Eulenburg pocket score.
[16] Presumably Hanslick means beginning at m. 40 in the Eulenburg pocket score; at m. 21 the same parody of the theme is played on clarinet in C (but in the distance).

rightly boast that Mozart recognized your musical insight. You are
no less entitled to boast that you recognized Berlioz's genius!

Eduard Hanslik.

V

Commentary

N THIS CHAPTER I provide some general remarks about Eduard Hanslick's essay "Ritter Berlioz in Prague" as a whole, and then add my comments on a few specific points.

This essay was one of the longest and most enthusiastic of the many articles published about Berlioz in the journals of Prague at the time of his visit there. That he nowhere mentions Hanslick's essay in his writings is one of the more puzzling aspects of our story. Perhaps he somehow became aware, while still in Prague, that young Hanslick had already begun to have second thoughts about him and his music.

The essay appeared in *Ost und West* in two instalments, 22 and 24 January 1846. It is in two parts, but these, as is often the case with serialized articles, do not correspond to the division into instalments. Hanslick does not provide separate headings for the two parts, but the division is clearly indicated: it comes on our p. 59 at the printer's rule,[1] with a paraphrase of Hanslick's epigraph from *King Lear*: "No, you cannot touch him for coining; he is the King himself." The second part is the review proper of Hector Berlioz's concert at the Sophieninselsaal on 19 January 1846.

The first part of the essay, and much of the second, must have been written well in advance of the concert, perhaps even prior to Berlioz's arrival in Prague, despite its opening words: "I have just come from the first of the Berlioz concerts." There would not have been time for the whole essay to have been written, edited, and set in type (by hand, of course) between the day of the concert and the days of publication, even if the author had not been busy going around with Berlioz as interpreter. The first part reads as if it had been thrashed out over coffee by the

---

[1] The printer's rule is also in the original.

Davids at one of their *Bündeleien*; it is more self-consciously literary (i.e. Jean-Paulian) than the second part, Hanslick's review of the concert. Much of this latter part is written in a chaste and subdued style compared to the first.

Eduard Hanslick was not at this time a beginner in the business of writing musical notices and reviews. He had been writing them for more than a year, beginning with the issue of *Prag* dated 18 November 1844, while still in his teens. The editor of *Ost und West* and *Prag* was Rudolf Glaser, a Skriptor at the Prague University Library. Young as Hanslick was at the time, he was not the youngest person Glaser took on as a contributor to his pages; the poet Alfred Meißner began writing for *Ost und West* a few years earlier, at the age of fifteen.

Hanslick wrote in his autobiography, decades later, that his friends in Prague were in 1846 as delighted by this essay as he in later years was embarrassed by the recollection of its immaturity and its euphoric tone.[2] It was to be expected that Hanslick would outgrow the euphoria, but not that he would he outgrow it so abruptly: "Ritter Berlioz in Prague" appeared in January 1846; in April 1847, a mere fifteen months later, an article by Hanslick appeared in a Viennese journal in which he virtually contradicted all his laudatory statements about Berlioz as musical poet and painter in the earlier essay. In the 1847 article Hanslick says that for Berlioz "music is not autonomous, not music in the strict sense of the word, i.e. a spontaneous play of tones in beautiful configurations."[3] The claim that music is "a spontaneous play of tones in beautiful configurations" is a version of Hanslick's central thesis in his book *Vom Musikalisch-Schönen* (first edition 1854); it expresses a conviction to which he adhered for the rest of his life, against powerful opposition.

Nobody acquainted with Hanslick only through his mature writings will be prepared for the essay "Ritter Berlioz in Prague," so opposite is it in content and tone to the formalistic and Apollinian aesthetical views customarily attributed to him. It represents, however, an important step in Hanslick's lifelong striving after solutions to theoretical problems

---

[2] Hanslick, *Leben*, vol. 1, p. 59.
[3] Eduard Hanslick, "Dr. Alfred Julius Becher," *Wiener Bote: Beilage zu den Sonntagsblätter*, vol. 6, no. 15 (11 April 1847), p. 123.

relating to the role of the feelings, and of any kind of extramusical content, in music.

We move now to my comments on specific points in Hanslick's "Ritter Berlioz in Prague."

p. 53, title: Ritter Berlioz

"Ritter" is a German translation of the French "Chevalier," to which Berlioz became entitled on 10 May 1839 when the Cross of the Legion of Honour was conferred upon him. He received few honours of any kind in his lifetime.

p. 53, ll. 7–16: realm of musical poetry . . . a great poet in musical sounds.

In this opening paragraph there is an undercurrent of double meanings not reproducible in English. We read that Berlioz is a "Tondichter," i.e. a poet in musical sounds, or equally, a joiner-together (com-poser) of sounds. "Realm of musical poetry" in this paragraph translates Hanslick's phrase "Gebiet der musikalischen Dichtung," which obviously has more to do with "poetry" in the familiar English sense of the word than with the artistic assembling of musical sounds (although the Greek *poíēsis*, from which "poetry" derives, has more to do with the latter than with the former). Hanslick's paragraph concludes with the exclamation that Berlioz is "ein großer Dichter!" which could mean that he is a great poet, but not exclusively in the pure literary sense; hence my elucidation: "a great poet in musical sounds."

A "Tondichter" could be either or both (*a*) a person who tells a story not in words but in music; (*b*) a person who puts musical sounds together, combines them into an artistic unity with no literary content. Nobody ever doubted that Berlioz qualifies under (*a*); Hanslick in this essay, and other contemporary and subsequent admirers of Berlioz, have felt obliged to insist that he qualifies under both.

p. 53, ll. 12–13: Guelphs and Ghibellines

These were the two great parties in medieval Italian politics. The Guelphs supported the Pope against the Emperor, the Ghibellines the Emperor against the Pope. They are here to be regarded as something like Swift's Big Endians and Little Endians, or W.S. Gilbert's little liber*als* and little conserva*tives*. In an essay of 1834 Hector Berlioz writes what he refers to as an old proverb: "In the arts one must take sides; there is no middle ground."[4]

p. 54, ll. 20–21: **without comprehension there can be no pleasure**
   Eight years later Hanslick wrote: "Without mental activity, there can be no aesthetical pleasure whatever." This was in his book *Vom Musikalisch-Schönen*, which I cite in my own translation.[5] One of the many rewards of studying the essay "Ritter Berlioz in Prague" is to see ideas beginning to take shape which were eventually given full treatment in that book. Other examples are pointed out in these comments.

p. 54, ll. 21–24: **intellectually and sensuously stimulating**
In his *On the Musically Beautiful*, Hanslick gives these various names, including "the aesthetical" and "the elemental" respectively. Their interrelationships are worked out in Chapters 4 and 5 of that book.

p. 54, l. 29–p. 55, l. 2: **musically beautiful**
   Here, so far as I know, is Hanslick's first published use of "Musikalisch-Schönen," the term he uses for one of the central concepts of his book, as the title suggests. That the musically beautiful is accessible only to musically trained and cultivated persons is one of the main themes in his book, and one of the reasons for the book's being condemned by some critics. Berlioz took a similar view in certain of his early writings;[6] it is likely that Hanslick was influenced by these writings, as well as by his conversations with Berlioz in Prague.

p. 56, l. 3: **homage to the new King**
There is something poignant in Hanslick's frequent use of terms relating to monarchs in describing Berlioz, both here in "Ritter Berlioz in Prague" and in his autobiography. At some level of consciousness

---

[4] Hector Berlioz, "Rossini's 'William Tell'" in Oliver Strunk, *Source Readings in Music History* (New York: Norton, 1950), p. 809.
[5] Hanslick, *Musically Beautiful* , p. 64.
[6] For example, see Strunk, *Readings*, pp. 808, 817, 825.

Hanslick, apparently, considers Berlioz to be mad like Lear, or on his way to becoming so. Is there more to Hanslick's choice of epigraph than meets the eye?

p. 56, l. 13: anonymity is for the hangman

In his review of Berlioz's *King Lear* Overture, A.W. Ambros said the same thing in different words: "In the heading of this essay I have not taken refuge behind a Flamin or a Victor, an Albanio, a Leitgeber, or the mask of any other pseudonym, but have written my real name exactly, like a sign over a portal."[7] These remarks of Hanslick and Ambros tell us much about the common (and, for generations of later scholars, confusing) practice of using ciphers and pseudonyms, especially for writings of a controversial nature.

p. 56, ll. 23–24: A gigantic mind requires a gigantic body.

Of Beethoven's Ninth Symphony Robert Schumann wrote in his essay on Berlioz's *Symphonie fantastique*: "The gigantic idea needed a giant's body" (Edward T. Cone's translation).[8] Hanslick's debt in "Ritter Berlioz in Prague" to Schumann's essay is obvious throughout.

p. 56, l. 26–p. 57, l. 5: the Romantic principle

This is popularized Hegelianism such as we find also in Hanslick's *King Lear* review (Chapter II above), and in his book *On the Musically Beautiful* (see pp. 20–21, note 5).

p. 58n, Hanslick's footnote: Berlioz's *bête noire*, the piano transcription

Schumann, in his essay on Berlioz, says that he was acquainted with the *Symphonie fantastique* only through Liszt's piano transcription. He wrote: "This piano arrangement is certainly unique and must be recommended as such to those who wish to learn the rare art of

---

[7] Ambros, [here "Jur. Dr. . . . aus Prag"] "Die Ouverture . . ." vol. 5, no. 120 (7 October 1845), p. 478.

[8] For the full citation of Schumann's essay see Bibliography. For the quotation in English translation: Schumann, "A Symphony by Berlioz," in Cone, *Berlioz Fantastic Symphony*, p. 227. Hereinafter I quote Schumann's essay in this edition.

[9] Schumann in Cone, *Berlioz Fantastic Symphony*, p. 244.

symphonic performance; we feel it our duty to voice here our warmest recognition of the credit Liszt so well deserves."[9] This footnote of Hanslick's is perhaps influenced by remarks to him by Berlioz on the subject of piano transcriptions.[10]

p. 58, ll. 17–18: the redoubtable B. Gutt
Bernhard Gutt's words on the *King Lear* Overture are translated above, p. 5. The reader should keep an eye on Gutt because he emerges in our narrative from obscurity and ridicule to a position of importance as a major influence on the young Hanslick.

p. 59, l. 14: Proch
Heinrich Proch (1809–1878) is almost a stock figure with Hanslick, who produces Proch's name whenever he wants to point to a bad composer whose success with the public is an indication of the public's deplorable standard of musical taste.[11]

p. 60, l. 31–p. 61, l. 2: such fiddle-faddle
Hanslick puns, rather feebly, on the name of Heinrich Wilhelm Ernst (1814–1865) and the German adjective "ernst," which translates "serious, earnest." H. W. Ernst was a disciple of Paganini; both were friends of Berlioz. Ernst, like his master, composed a "Carnival of Venice" as a display piece for solo violin. Both "Carnivals" were excessively familiar to the musical public of Prague. When a cellist from Warsaw named Kossowski came to Prague with yet another "Carnival of Venice," some of the local music critics ridiculed it. Dr. Kossowski's visit to Prague caused a minor musical sensation there at around the time of Berlioz's arrival on 14 January 1846.

Kossowski took part in three concerts: 3, 6, and 12 January. On 3 January he played one piece for cello with piano, and three for cello with string sextet. These latter were composed by himself; one of them was his "Carnival of Venice" thus arranged. *Bohemia*, in the issue of 6 January, reviewed Kossowski's performance with mild approval; the reviewer

---

[10] Berlioz, *Mémoires*, vol. 1, pp. 148–49.
[11] Hanslick, *Musically Beautiful*, pp. 18, 106 n. 6.

was Bernhard Gutt, who was one of that journal's two co-editors (the other was Franz Klutschak).

In the second of his concerts, 6 January, Kossowski played his "Carnival of Venice," this time without accompaniment. In musically conservative Prague, an unaccompanied performance on cello would have been regarded as a mere novelty, a stunt, something like juggling on a tightrope. The reviewer for *Bohemia* was, once again, Bernhard Gutt, whom young Eduard Hanslick had referred to ironically the previous year as "redoubtable" in his "Ritter Berlioz in Prague." Perhaps sharpening his pen in anticipation of Berlioz's first concert, the date of which had not yet been announced, Gutt wrote:

> Herr Kossowski played a solo of his own composition. A concert piece for unaccompanied cello is all but an impossibility; Herr Kossowski did not bring it off. A more pointless, more muddled composition we have scarcely ever heard; it was originality gone mad. Certainly Herr Kossowski proved himself to be an excellent player, but the whole piece displeased. The concert was extremely poorly attended.[12]

In the next issue of *Bohemia* an announcement of Kossowski's third recital in Prague (on 12 January, but *Ost und West* announced it for the 11th) appeared. *Bohemia's* announcement says, in part:

> In fairness to Kossowski, it should be mentioned that he has many times performed his concert piece for unaccompanied cello with great success, thereby proving the possibility of such an undertaking, contrary to the opinion expressed by a reviewer in the preceding issue of this journal.[13]

Bohemia's reviewer at Kossowski's third concert was not Bernhard Gutt, but someone signing himself "R.S.", whom later we shall find to be in sharp opposition to Gutt on the subject of Berlioz's music. "R.S." wrote:

> This journal has already commented upon Herr Kossowski's artistic importance. We need only add that this time he gave even more pleasure than he did at his first concert. ... In particular, Herr

---

[12] Bernhard Gutt [here "G."], "Concert der Dem. Sophie Bohrer," *Bohemia*, vol. 19, no. 4 (9 January 1846), n.p.
[13] *Bohemia*, vol. 19, no. 5 (11 January 1846), n.p.

Kossowski's harmonics are the most perfect we have ever heard on the cello, although we make no secret of our preference for singing rather than tooting on this beautiful instrument. Also, the time has come for the Messrs. Virtuosi to spare us Carnivals of Venice. Not only violins, but also cellos, bassoons, waldhorns and the rest, have had to put up with this carnival jollification. It would be a good thing to give them up for Lent, permanently.[14]

I make no secret of my suspicion that "R.S." is none other than Flamin, the Last (or Least) of the Davidsbündler, masquerading under the initials of the First, Robert Schumann. But of this there is more to come.

Ost und West's report on the third concert of Kossowski is signed "Dr. H.", perhaps Joseph Heller ("Obolus"). He wrote:

The "Carnival" received thunderous applause, which it richly deserved. This piece demonstrates the more spectacular side of the soloist's art, especially the fluent runs in harmonics, and the mellow singing on one string. Herr Kossowski was recalled three times after this piece, but he declined to repeat it.[15]

p. 61, ll. 12–13: pictorial-literary music

Few of Hanslick's contemporaries doubted that it is possible for composers to produce tone-paintings and tone-poems; in 1846, when he wrote "Ritter Berlioz in Prague," Hanslick shared this view. One year later he denied in print that music can reproduce anything concrete in tonal combinations.[16] Eight years later he denied that composers can represent in music a definite content.[17] From this last view he never

---

[14] "R.S." [August Wilhelm Ambros?], "Zweites Concert des Herrn Kossowski," *Bohemia*, vol. 19, no. 7 (16 January 1846), n.p. On 15 March 1845 the famous violin virtuoso H.W. Ernst performed in Prague, not for the first time, his own composition "Carnival of Venice." Hanslick twitted him good-naturedly for it. Eduard Hanslick [here "Ed–d."], "Konzert am 15 März zum Vortheil des Privatvereins zur Unterstützung der Prager Hausarmen," *Prag*, no. 44, (17 March 1845), p. 174.

[15] "Dr. H." [Joseph Heller?], "Prager Nachrichten," *Ost und West*, vol. 10, no. 6 (15 January 1846), p. 24.

[16] Hanslick, "Becher," p. 123.

[17] Hanslick, *Musically Beautiful*, p. 35. In the first German edition (1854) the passage is on p. 41.

swerved, although he stood almost alone among musical theoreticians against the prevailing view of the matter.

p. 61, l. 23–p. 62, l.7: Concluding the program . . . mad with love.
This is the most Schumannian paragraph in "Ritter Berlioz in Prague." Schumann plays upon "She!" rather than "You!" and continues: "Tasso was thus driven into the madhouse." Schumann says that Berlioz's love for Harriet Smithson is "all written there in the first movement with drops of blood."[18]

p. 62, ll. 8–11: Professor F[étis] in Brussels . . . letter of safe conduct
Berlioz had an ambivalent relationship with François-Joseph Fétis, who was, among other things, founder and editor of *Revue musicale*. In the issue of 1 February 1835 Fétis published a harsh critique, written by himself, of the *Symphonie fantastique*. Robert Schumann published a German translation of this in his *Neue Zeitschrift für Musik*; his famous essay on Berlioz is his reply to Fétis. The critique by Fétis is the "letter of safe conduct" to which Hanslick refers.[19]

p. 62, ll. 25–28: narrative descriptions
Robert Schumann objected even more strenuously than did Hanslick to Berlioz's printed "program" for the *Symphonie fantastique*. "All Germany is happy to let him keep it," Schumann wrote. "Such signposts always have something unworthy and charlatan-like about them! . . . The German, with his delicacy of feeling and his aversion to personal revelation, dislikes having his thoughts so rudely directed."[20] "R.S." in *Bohemia* objected likewise: "In Paris, the great metropolis, where everybody tries to outdo everyone else, such a prop is certainly needed to grab the attention of the audience; but in Germany a few introductory words about the subject of the symphony, and simple captions to the individual movements, would have been enough."[21]

---

[18] Schumann in Cone, *Berlioz Fantastic Symphony*, p. 224.

[19] François-Joseph Fétis, trans. Edward T. Cone, "Critical Analysis," in Cone, *Berlioz Fantastic Symphony*, pp. 215–20. The "nightmare" is on p. 217.

[20] Schumann in Cone, *Berlioz Fantastic Symphony*, p. 246.

[21] "R.S." [August Wilhelm Ambros?], "Concert des Herrn Hektor Berlioz," *Bohemia*, vol. 19, no. 10 (23 January 1846), n.p.

p. 64, l. 32–p. 65, l. 2: **Pragers!**
Mozart's words "my Pragers understand me!" turn up frequently in our narrative, but documentary evidence that he actually uttered them is not easy to find. While investigating the poet and journalist Alfred Meißner for the present work I came across a volume, edited by him, of papers selected from the literary remains of his grandfather August Gottlieb Meißner (1753–1807), who was professor of aesthetics at Prague University. A.G. Meißner attended the performance in the Ständetheater in 1787 at which Mozart exclaimed those words; Alfred Meißner handed his grandfather's wonderful eyewitness account along to us:

> On the morning of 29 October 1787 there were posters on the street corners announcing that *Don Giovanni* would be given that evening. . . .
>
> This opera was going to open the winter season at the Ständetheater, and the auspices were the brightest possible. We knew that Mozart had written it with Prague in mind.
>
> The procession of carriages began as early as half past five. Soon there was a great traffic jam. We saw women, dressed to the nines, abandoning their carriages and trying to pick their way to the entrance through a sea of mud. Upon entering the auditorium, they found the galleries and the parterre already filled. The gallery was a terrifying sight, the people packed in cheek by jowl, and those in the back rows, clinging to the iron rail that ran from pillar to pillar, seemed on the brink of falling upon the rows below. Through the excited buzzing of the crowd one could barely make out the cry of the lackey who went around selling beer and sausages to the insatiables in the Gods, while "Lemonade!" resounded in the lower regions. . . .
>
> The moment Mozart appeared on the podium he was greeted by vigorous applause which he acknowledged in every direction; he quickly gave the downbeat, and there sounded forth those mighty chords, as if from the spirit world, shaking the human heart to the core, which are, as it were, the bronze portals to this masterwork.
>
> Three hours later an opera, whose like had never been heard in the whole realm of music, came to the end of its first performance. The dissolute pagan, who defied God and all His angels, had gone down into the eternal fiery pit. A world of pleasure, wantonness, horror, lamentation, and despair, such as only Mozart could portray, had been

Fig. 14. ALFRED MEIßNER, poet and journalist
Began writing for *Ost und West* at the age of fifteen. His grandfather attended the first performance of *Don Giovanni* in 1787.

made to unfold before the listeners, and the reward was tremendous applause. On this evening Mozart spoke those words which have become so famous: "My Pragers understand me!"—a saying that generations of Pragers will always revere.[22]

p. 65, last line: Hanslik

This is the spelling with which Eduard's father, Josef Adolf Hanslik, signed his own writings. "Ritter Berlioz in Prague" is the first publication to which Eduard Hanslick attached his full signature, but in that spelling. Previously he signed his reviews "Ed–d." For the remainder of the year 1846 he used "Hanslik," then in the following year he wavered between the two spellings of his surname, then settled upon "Hanslick," interspersed by "Ed.-H." or, on special occasions, "Renatus," his Davidsbündler name. Perhaps he considered "Hanslick" more Germanic, and hence more chic, than the Bohemian "Hanslik."

---

[22] Alfred Meißner, *Rococo-Bilder: Nach Aufzeichnungen meines Grossvaters* (Gumbinnen: Krauseneck, 1871), pp. 113–15.

VI

Berliozstadt Prag

FRENZIED" MAY SEEM too strong a word, but something close to it would describe the reception given Hector Berlioz by the musical public of Prague in January 1846. Mozart's *Don Giovanni* had its première performance at the Ständetheater in 1787 before an enraptured audience; since then Prague had been known to German musicians, sometimes ironically, as "Mozart-town" (*die Mozartstadt*). In 1846 Prague became Berlioz-town.[1]

Berlioz's ovations in Prague were due in large part to deliberate manipulation of public opinion by means of the press. This, I have little doubt, was part of a campaign waged by August Wilhelm Ambros and his Prager Davidsbündler to liberate their city from the conservative programming of its concert and opera managements, committed as these latter were to the Mozartian repertoire.

Like specialized musical journals such as Robert Schumann's *Neue Zeitschrift für Musik* in Leipzig (from which I quoted at length in Chapter I above), many newspapers in the German-speaking countries had been publishing items concerning Berlioz and his music for some years, particularly since he embarked on his first German tour in 1842. In Prague the publicity reached its peak at around the turn of 1845/46. From November to January the three journals we have been consulting (*Bohemia, Ost und West,* and *Prag*) published between them more than a dozen items about Berlioz: accounts of his triumphs in Vienna, of his whole career; announcements of his intention to come to Prague, of his

---

[1] Ottokar Hostinsky, "Musik in Böhmen," in Rudolf, Archduke (convener), *Die österreichische-ungarische Monarchie in Wort und Bild,* 24 vols. (Vienna: Hof- und Staatsdruckerei, 1896), vol. 10, pp. 40–41. Hostinsky says that Berlioz was officially recognized in Prague when, in 1847, he was made an Honorary Member of the Prague Conservatory, along with Franz Liszt.

arrival there from Vienna, and the like. *Ost und West* carried a biographical essay on Berlioz by Ambros;[2] *Bohemia* made a premature announcement of a concert in Prague by Berlioz, allegedly to be held on 14 December 1845, one month before he actually arrived there;[3] *Ost und West* (but not *Bohemia*) published a notice stating that this concert had been cancelled due to the overwhelming demand in Vienna for another concert there by Berlioz.[4] It can hardly be doubted that these items, or some of them, were planted by the Davidsbündler.

Describing events in Prague on 19 January 1846, the day of Berlioz's first concert in Prague, Katinka Emingerová wrote:

> The experts tell us that the day of Berlioz's first concert is a particularly significant one in the musical history of Prague. The turnout at his concert was absolutely without precedent, according to *Bohemia*.[5] That same evening there was a performance of Shakespeare's *The Taming of the Shrew* at the Ständetheater, beautifully prepared, but it played to an almost empty house. *Bohemia*'s drama critic sighed: "Blame it on Berlioz's concert!"[6]

In his autobiography (1894) Eduard Hanslick wrote:

> There had never been anything in Prague like the excitement stirred up by Berlioz's concerts there. Ambros reported on them in *Bohemia*, while I, using my full signature for the first time, wrote a long essay on Berlioz for *Ost und West*.[7]

---

[2] August Wilhelm Ambros [here "Dr. August Ambros"], "Hektor Berlioz," *Ost und West*, vol. 9, no. 99 (12 December 1845), pp. 393–94. Another biographical account is unsigned, but may also be by Ambros: [August Wilhelm Ambros?] "Hektor Berlioz," *Bohemia*, vol. 18, no. 145 (2 December 1845), n.p.

[3] *Bohemia*, vol. 18, no. 148 (9 December 1845), n.p.

[4] *Ost und West*, no. 197 (10 December 1845), p. 788.

[5] "R.S." [August Wilhelm Ambros?], "Concert des Herrn Hektor Berlioz," *Bohemia*, vol. 19, no. 10 (23 January 1846), n.p.

[6] Emingerová, "Hector Berlioz à Prague," p. 174. I have found no trace in *Bohemia* of the sigh. The Shakespeare production mentioned here took place not on the evening of Berlioz's first concert, as Emingerová states, but on the evening before, according to *Bohemia*, vol. 19, no. 11 (25 January 1846), n.p.

[7] Hanslick, *Leben*, vol. 1, p. 59.

The long essay by himself to which Hanslick here refers is "Ritter Berlioz in Prague," the centrepiece of the present volume. A report by Ambros of Berlioz's concert of 31 March 1846 appeared in *Bohemia*, the issue of 5 April 1846, over the signature "–29.".[8] As "August Wilhelm Ambros" he wrote a pair of "open letters to the music lovers of Prague" for the *Prager Zeitung;*[9] but these are not reviews, merely propaganda for the Berlioz concerts, addressed to unmusical readers with the intention of arousing their interest in the more sensational aspects of Berlioz's career and music.

But the plot, as elsewhere in our narrative, thickens. *Bohemia's* review of the first Berlioz concert (19 January 1846) is signed "R.S."[10] We must look carefully at "R.S.", because hardly anything in our narrative is as it seems, and because musical journalists of that time and place loved their little games with pseudonyms and ciphers. "R.S." makes a few minor appearances in *Bohemia* at around the time of Berlioz's visit; we have already met him in one of my comments in the preceding chapter. He is the one who likes cellos to sing rather than tootle, and who thinks composer-virtuosi should give up Carnivals of Venice for Lent. The initials "R.S." (if, indeed, they are initials) do not match the name of any musical journalist in Prague at that time with whose writings I am acquainted. But perhaps a few selections from his review will strike a familiar note.

> It seems to us almost a dream that we have at last seen and heard the much-admired, much-anathematized composer in person; the 19th day of January 1846 must stand out as one of the most noteworthy dates in the artistic annals of Prague. We cheerfully grant that, on this day, many things turned out quite otherwise than as we expected. Led astray by ridicule in the journals (and we must now say that this ridicule was undeserved), we expected to in find Berlioz's music a mixture of contrived *coups de théâtre* and tiresome distractions, an incomprehen-

---

[8] August Wilhelm Ambros [here "–29."], under heading "Theater," *Bohemia*, vol. 19, no. 42 (5 April 1846), n.p. For the decoding of this cipher see above, p. 13, note 35.

[9] Ambros, "Sendschreiben," pp. 127–28; "Zweites Sendschreiben," p. 161. Emingerová says that Ambros had a review in *Pražské Noviny*, but she provides no details. "Hector Berlioz à Prague," p. 174.

[10] "R.S." [Ambros?], "Concert des Herrn Hektor Berlioz," n.p.

sible jumble of sounds interspersed with occasional lucid bits. Instead, one musical glory after another soared before us in luminous magnificence. We expected a partly bewildered, partly horrified audience, but instead, the people listened to the music with almost breathless attentiveness, and at the end of every piece the applause was like thunder; indeed, the *Roman Carnival* Overture and the "Pilgrims' March" were encored. In short (hear, hear!) Berlioz enjoyed an overwhelming triumph in musical Prague.[11]

This writing is pure Ambrosia and is in the succession from Jean Paul by way of Robert Schumann. Also, for whom else in Prague but Ambros would a Berliozian triumph in that city have been like a dream come true? Perhaps everyone expected a partly bewildered, partly horrified audience, but only Ambros had already put it that way (or nearly so) in print, in his *King Lear* review quoted in Chapter I above. And surely only Ambros had the cheek to interject the parliamentary "hear, hear!"

"R.S." quotes other writers who have compared Berlioz with Beethoven, and continues the comparison:

Beethoven's audacious play of imagination is tempered by an awe-inspiring sagacity and discretion; Berlioz, on the other hand, lets himself go. He takes to the air and flies to wherever his imagination carries him, but always to his goal: sometimes in a straight line, with the strength and sureness of the eagle; sometimes in an elegant curve; sometimes in a peculiar zigzag.[12]

"R.S." enthuses over the quality of the orchestral performances:

The performances of all the pieces were the best evidence of how splendid are the resources and musicians of Prague. The orchestra of the Conservatory supplemented that of the Imperial Ständetheater; in the playing together of these two assemblages we could not help thinking about the "We are famous heroes" of the Spartan men, and the "But we will nevertheless surpass you wherever we can" of the Spartan youths.[13]

If I am correct in my surmise that "R.S." is August Wilhelm Ambros, what was he trying to convey with those two letters?

---

[11] Ibid., n.p.
[12] Ibid., n.p.
[13] Ibid., n.p.

My conjecture is that Flamin, the Last (or Least) of the Davidsbündler, was having a little charade with the initials of the First, Robert Schumann, who, under the pseudonyms "Eusebius" and "Florestan," was the author of the first major study in German of a work by Hector Berlioz, namely the *Symphonie fantastique*. This conjecture may seem far-fetched, but not if we consider the extent to which the Prague musical journalists exchanged elaborate jokes in print, sometimes cryptically. Ambros, whom Hanslick considered capable of almost anything preposterous, was capable of this masquerade.

In a letter dated 21 January 1846 Berlioz wrote:

> My first concert enjoyed a success of the most extraordinary spontane-ity and enthusiasm. All my Prague friends tell me that their city has never displayed such a musical frenzy. Three of my pieces were encored; Dr. Ambros and Kittl tell me that this has never before occurred here for works of instrumental music. In particular, the "Scène au champs" and the "Marche au Supplice" produced remarkable impressions. The playing of the instrumentalists seemed to me excep-tionally fine, the orchestra being made up of artists from the Ständetheater combined with the best pupils of the Conservatory. I was astonished by the swiftness of their comprehension and by the sheer competence of most of the players. . . . Kittl comes along to the rehearsals, bringing with him his classes from the Conservatory so they may learn the art of breaking new ground, of hacking a path through the underbrush.
>
> As for Dr. Ambros, his happiness is so complete that it is contagious; it would have been worth my while to come to Prague if only to behold his delight. Tomaschek has delivered his verdict: he is one-third for me, two-thirds against. He says that I'm not completely mad, just partly so.
>
> When I arrived here they told me about the hostility of a musical journalist named Got or God or whatever [Bernhard Gutt], who tilted at the *King Lear* Overture a year ago and put his reputation on the line to prove that nobody can have the faintest idea of what I'm doing. I don't know yet what effect my concert has had upon his opinion, but I'm not losing much sleep over this.[14]

---

[14] Berlioz, *Correspondance*, vol. 3, p. 307.

Bernhard Gutt's article on Berlioz appeared in *Bohemia* in four parts over three instalments, 27 and 30 January and 1 February 1846.[15] On the latter date, Berlioz was already away from Prague on his conducting tour; but it was expected that he would return a few weeks later to conduct his *Romeo and Juliet* Symphony, as indeed he did. Gutt, therefore, was in a position to review together the first three Berlioz concerts and to report in full on his triumphant January days there. Gutt's article, thought generally negative in its assessment of the music, is fair-minded and restrained, certainly nothing for Berlioz to lose sleep over. Gutt's personal views did not prevent his publishing in *Bohemia* several extremely favourable articles on Berlioz by other hands, as he took pains to point out.

"I do not want to judge Berlioz, merely to understand him," Gutt wrote. He reiterated in modified form his earlier view of the *King Lear* Overture: "While there is music in it, it is not in itself music." In words with which Hanslick could have agreed one year later, Gutt continues: "The composer works from the centre of the musical idea toward the circumference of the tonal structure."[16] This is Gutt's way of denying that the composer of music is in any way a poet or a painter in sounds. In this he was opposed to most of his colleagues among musical journalists in the German-speaking countries of Europe, including (but only for the moment) Eduard Hanslick.

For contrast I shall quote from an essay which appeared in the *Prager Zeitung* around the time Gutt's article on Berlioz appeared in *Bohemia*. It has the title "Yet another word about Hector Berlioz by a nonmusician,"

---

[15] Bernhard Gutt [here "B.G."], "Hector Berlioz," *Bohemia*, vol. 19, no. 12 (27 January 1846), n.p.; no. 13 (30 January 1846), n.p.; no. 14 (1 February 1846), n.p. Gutt died in 1849; a tribute to him by Ambros included these words: "Critical opinions of Berlioz were more sharply divided than those of any other artist. On the one hand he was idolized, on the other reviled; precisely those criticisms that sought an intermediate position between these extremes were the most inept. Gutt removed himself from all these, and set forth his own view. It went right to the heart of the matter and was moreover so straightforward and obvious that to the reader it seemed as if he had arrived at the same view all on his own." August Wilhelm Ambros [here "A.W. Ambros"], "Bernhard Gutt als Musiker (Beschluß)," *Bohemia*, vol. 22, no. 81 (5 April 1849), n.p. (This is the concluding part of a three-part essay on Bernhard Gutt by Ambros.)

[16] Gutt [here "B.G."], "Berlioz" (27 January 1846), n.p.

and is signed "*9*", perhaps a version of "29", i.e. August Wilhelm Ambros. "*9*" tells us that, at Berlioz's birth, Mother Nature handed him the seven musical tones (i.e. the degrees of the diatonic scales) and said: "Here, go and work miracles with them." After a few lines on the subject of genius as as natural gift, he continues:

> Hector Berlioz is a painter. His is not musical painting; it is rather painterly music. He is a painter of the Italian school: he sat at the easel of a Titian, and learned from him how to paint with the richest palette. His colours glow; indeed they may seem garish to delicate eyes. His imagination is tropical: its products are gigantic and decked out in the most luxuriant hues. Would anyone quarrel with Nature for giving the panther its colourfully spotted coat? Would anyone call her prodigal for outfitting the parrot in such plumage? . . .
>
> Hector Berlioz is a tone-poet. He has the sensitivity and the inventiveness of a poet. There passes before him a whole artistic life with its joys and sorrows. He tells us about it in musical sounds, and causes it to unfold before us in all its eventfulness.[17]

The journalistic campaign to arouse public interest in the Berlioz concerts was only one factor. Many years later, Eduard Hanslick pointed out that in the Prague of 1846 everything was ripe for the music Berlioz brought with him.

> Time and place could scarcely have been more propitious for Berlioz. A breath of fresh air was blowing through the musical life of the old city on the Moldau, bringing with it an enthusiastic ambitiousness, receptiveness, and discernment. For too long had Pragers been under the spell of a hidebound classicism imposed by their most illustrious and influential musical institution, the Prague Conservatory, under its otherwise very competent director, Dionys Weber. He was so conservative that he acknowledged only the first three of Beethoven's sympho-

---

[17] August Wilhelm Ambros [here "*9*"], "Auch ein Wort über Berlioz von einem Nichtmusikalischen," *Prager Zeitung*, no. 16 (27 January 1846), p. 214. Presumably the previous "Nichtmusikalischer" to whom the "Auch" refers was "M.", the author of an essay "Hektor Berlioz" in *Ost und West*, vol. 10, no. 43 (11 April 1846), pp. 171–72. "M." claims to be a nonmusician. My own conjecture is that "M." is the poet Alfred Meißner, who met Berlioz at a party on the Sophieninsel in January 1846. Alfred Meißner, *Geschichte meines Lebens*, 3rd ed., 2 vols. (Vienna and Teschen: Prochaska, 1884), pp. 137–38.

nies as symphonies. For too long had Pragers firmly refused to be weaned from their diet of Haydn, Mozart, Spohr, and Onslow, and had become almost unbearably arrogant and reactionary in their awareness of the Mozartian accolade: "The Pragers understand me!" The ice was broken when Kittl took over as director of the Conservatory: Beethoven's later works and Mendelssohn's orchestral poems made audiences sit up and take notice; people soon became acquainted with Gade and Hiller, and ready to take a chance on Schumann's *Das Paradies und die Peri*, and, for that matter, on the *King Lear* Overture by Hector Berlioz.[18]

In the Prague journals of January 1846 there was uncertainty regarding Berlioz's plans for the near future. *Ost und West* announced on 24 January that Berlioz would give his second and final concert the next day, listing the works to be performed, and concluding: "We regret that this inspired artist is leaving us so soon";[19] we, of course, know that this was not the final concert of Berlioz's sojourn in Prague.[20] *Bohemia* announced the second concert and, like *Ost und West*, stated that this would be Berlioz's final concert in Prague.[21] Presumably Berlioz was himself the main source of this uncertainty. He, along with Recio and Ambros, and perhaps the young student Hanslick, would have wanted to assess the response to his first concert with care. Was the wildly enthusiastic applause merely a flash in the pan, never to be repeated? Did it seem to justify a second concert? A third? In all things there is a danger of outstaying one's welcome; for a performer the danger is that he will find himself playing to a small and jaded audience; this can be a devastating experience. So there may have been considerable backing and filling on Berlioz's part, with Ambros giving premature and incomplete announcements of forthcoming events to the press; he had been doing this sort of thing since early December. A veteran journalist, Ambros knew well the uses of misinformation in the press to arouse interest in some person or cause. The Davids were promoting a person in aid of what they considered to be an exalted cause, to judge by some

---

[18] Hanslick, *Concertsaal*, p. 483. See also Ludvová, "Zur Biographie Eduard Hanslicks," pp. 41–42.
[19] *Ost und West*, vol. 10, no. 10 (24 January 1846), p. 40.
[20] Berlioz's sixth and final concert was on 17 April 1846.
[21] *Bohemia*, vol. 19, no. 10 (23 January 1846), n.p.

Fig. 15. Poster announcing Berlioz's third concert in Prague (Ständetheater, 27 January 1846); the fifth movement of the *Symphonie fantastique* is not mentioned, and was not played on this occasion.

of Hanslick's more high-flown utterances in "Ritter Berlioz in Prague" ("In partisan matters a man has to put his whole person on the line; and, where a noble cause is at stake, anonymity is for the hangman."). The programs of Berlioz's January concerts did not vary much from one to the next. There was insatiable demand for the *Symphonie fantastique*, which the January audiences heard without the final movement; also for the "Pilgrims' March" from *Harold in Italy*, and a few others.

If I have it right, there were some amusing goings-on with the *Fantastique*. The reader will recall that Hanslick, in "Ritter Berlioz in Prague," reported that the composer was judicious and sensitive enough to omit the fifth movement ("Songe d'une nuit du Sabbat") at his first concert; "it presses hard against the limits of the aesthetical," sniffed the young critic.

Nevertheless, from the advance notices it seems that Berlioz announced his intention to include the final movement in the program of his second concert, 25 January, but from the reviews it is evident that he again deleted it. He did not play the "Songe" until his fourth concert, 31 March. Why the delay? Had Hanslick's reservations about the piece weighed upon Berlioz's conscience and prevented him from playing the *Fantastique* in its entirety?

Hanslick provides the dénouement in his autobiography.

> I did not attend the final concert [it was in fact the fourth of six], in which Berlioz performed the fifth movement of the *Symphonie fantastique*, which was routinely omitted everywhere else. At just that particular time an opportunity presented itself for me to go to Vienna. I had a greater desire to become acquainted with that city than with the "Ronde de Sabbat" by Berlioz. In Vienna I had the delightful surprise of receiving from Berlioz the following whimsical note about this performance: "Henry IV wrote: 'Go and hang yourself, Crillon! We defeated them at Arques and you were not there!' Our 'Sabbat' was performed last Tuesday [31 March 1846]; I shall not urge you to hang yourself, because it went very well. Best wishes. Come back to us soon."[22]

---

[22] Hanslick, *Leben*, vol. 1, pp. 59–60. Regarding Henry IV and Crillon: "Hang thyself, brave Grillon; we have fought at Arques, and thou wert not there. Vanquished or victorious, I am

Fig. 16. Poster announcing Berlioz's fourth concert in Prague (Ständetheater, 31 March 1846); the fifth movement of the *Symphonie fantastique* was played; Eduard Hanslick was in Vienna.

From this it seems that the "Songe" was at the limits, not of the aesthetical, as Hanslick wrote in his essay, but of the playable. The instrumentalists, excellent musicians though they were, in one rehearsal after another failed to get on top of the piece; so it was deleted at the last moment each time until the fourth concert. Hanslick, in his capacity as Berlioz's interpreter at rehearsals, must have despaired of its ever being ready for performance in Prague; by fleeing to Vienna he avoided what he considered an inevitable disaster.

However one interprets these events (and the foregoing is no more than an interpretation), they suggest a happy and comfortable relationship between the famous composer and the young student in Prague.

Hanslick's trip to Vienna was his Easter vacation. He took with him a letter of introduction from Berlioz to Franz Liszt; a quotation from this is the epigraph to the present volume.[23] Liszt now becomes a major figure in our narrative. He was kind to Hanslick in Vienna on that occasion;[24] a few days later he shared the limelight in Prague with Berlioz; and when Hanslick, in the autumn of that year (1846), wrote his extremely important essay on Richard Wagner's *Tannhäuser*, he borrowed for study a copy of the score previously given to Liszt by Wagner himself.

To refresh our memories: Berlioz's visit to Prague began on 14 January 1846, when he arrived there from Vienna; it ended with his departure on 18 or 19 April, with an interval from just after his third concert on 27 January until his return to Prague on 25 March; during this interval he conducted in Vienna, Budapest, and Breslau.

We return briefly to the January days immediately following Berlioz's first concert (19 January). No doubt there was a schedule of further rehearsals, and, for the famous composer and his "wife" Marie Recio, a

---

ever thine. (Signed) Henry." Marguerite de Lussan, trans. "a lady," rev. "Mr. Richardson," *The Life and Heroic Actions of Balba Berton, Chevalier de Grillon,* 2 vols. (London: Woodgate & Brooks, n.d.), vol. 2, p. 68.

[23] Berlioz, *Correspondance,* vol. 3, p. 330.

[24] Hanslick describes his first meeting with Liszt in *Leben,* vol. 1, pp. 81–83 and p. 100.

round of visits to fashionable homes. It was with just such occasions in mind that Berlioz always referred to Recio as "Madame Berlioz."[25]

Despite these many activities, Berlioz found time to write letters to various people, expressing his delight at his reception in Prague, as we have already seen. A few days after his departure for Vienna (27 or 28 January), he wrote from that city a letter to Kittl in Prague, concerning practical arrangements for the performance he expected to conduct there of his *Romeo and Juliet* Symphony. In this letter he asks Kittl to extend his greetings to Ambros, Hanslick, Gordigiani (professor of singing at the Prague Conservatory), and Hoffmann (presumably the director, not the music dealer).[26] He wrote to Ambros from Budapest two weeks later, expressing alarm that he had not received from Hoffmann confirmation that the choral parts of *Romeo and Juliet* had arrived safely in Prague, and again to Ambros in March, from Breslau, on matters relating to his next round of concerts in Prague, and sending personal greetings to Hanslick.[27] I have mentioned here only a few of the letters Berlioz wrote while on his interval of eight weeks away from Prague.

Eduard Hanslick wrote, early in the 1880s:

> In Prague, what stimulated and reinforced our enthusiasm for Berlioz's music was our personal contact with him, the impression we had of his amiable and noble personality. His artistic ideal occupied him to the exclusion of all else; the realization of it . . . was his sole aim and aspiration. In his art, whatever one makes of it nowadays, there was a sublime integrity: this man with the head of a Jupiter was far removed from everything selfish and petty. I can still respond to his personal grandeur and courage, and to certain beautiful passages in his music. But in my maturity I cannot revive the boundless enthusiasm I had for him in my youth in Prague.[28]

---

[25] Berlioz, *Correspondance*, vol. 3, p. 305: "M. et Madame Berlioz ont l'honneur de saluer madame la Comptesse de Schlick et de la remercier de son aimable invitation à laquelle ils se rendront avec empressement."

[26] Ibid., pp. 312–13.

[27] Ibid., pp. 316, 322.

[28] Hanslick, *Leben*, vol. 1, p. 60.

Fig. 17. Eduard Hanslick in his sixty-eighth year
In his maturity he could not revive the boundless enthusiasm he had for Berlioz in Prague.

VII

"O Praga! quando te aspiciam?"

 N HIS *Mémoires* Hector Berlioz wrote:

I gave six concerts in Prague, some of them in the Ständetheater and some in the Sophieninselsaal. To my great delight, Liszt was at my final concert, and there he heard my *Romeo and Juliet* Symphony for the first time. I had already played a few excerpts from this work in Prague, and these had not given rise to any violent controversy, perhaps because the work had by then been the subject of lively polemics in Vienna; in matters of musical taste, certainly, there is rivalry between the two cities.

The vocal performances were magnificent, barring a single mishap. The young person entrusted with the alto solo had never before sung solo in public. Despite her extreme nervousness, everything went well so long as she was supported by instruments or other voices. But in the Prologue, when she got to "Le jeune Roméo plaignant sa destinée," a real solo without any kind of accompaniment, her voice began to wobble and slip, until at the end of the sentence, where the harp comes in with an E major triad, she had arrived at some key nobody ever heard of, about one and a quarter tones below E. The harpist, Mademoiselle Claudius, who sat alongside the podium, hesitated, then whispered to me: "Should I play the E major chord?"

"Certainly," I replied. "We have to get out of this somehow."

So the E major triad rang forth inexorably, hissing and spluttering like a blob of molten lead dropped into a bucket of cold water. The poor little singer had a hard time getting on the right track; because she knew no French I couldn't fall back on my customary eloquence to reassure her. Fortunately she regained her *sang-froid* in time for the verse beginning "Premiers transports . . ." which she sang with spirit and irreproachable precision. Strakaty played the rôle of Friar Laurence to perfection, with just the right measure of unction and genuine feeling in the Finale.

On that day, after having encored several numbers, the audience demanded that we play yet another piece again, but the orchestra begged me not to concur. When the outcry persisted, Monsieur Mildner took out his watch and held it up in plain view to let everyone know that there would not be time to play it again, since there was to be an opera at seven o'clock that evening. This clever pantomime saved the day.

At the end, I asked Liszt (as my translator on that occasion) to thank the singers for me, since for the past three weeks they had been studying my choruses with the utmost devotion, and had sung them valiantly. But a few of them came forward on behalf of their comrades to invert the proposition: after a brief exchange in German, Liszt turned to me and said that his commission had been altered, and that it was these people who begged to thank me for the pleasure I had given them performing my music with them, and to express their joy that I was satisfied with their performance of it.

That was a splendid day for me. I have few memories to compare with it.[1]

The unfortunate alto on whose behalf the blob of molten lead was dropped into the bucket of cold water was "Fräul. Ržepka," according to *Ost und West* and *Bohemia*. She caught Berlioz's ear (and, no doubt, his famous roving eye) at the rehearsal he attended of the Sophienakademie on 16 January 1846. Perhaps he owed her a favour; perhaps there were no contralto soloists in the Opera at the Ständetheater whom he considered right for the part.[2]

The harpist, Anna Claudius, was a musician for whom Berlioz had an especially high regard. The foremost pupil of Elias Parish-Alvars (an Englishman known as "the Franz Liszt of the harp"), she was also a singer of considerable accomplishment, being frequently heard as soloist in performances of the Sophienakademie.[3]

---

[1] Berlioz, *Mémoires*, vol. 2, pp. 241–43.

[2] Berlioz, *Correspondance*, vol. 3, p. 313. According to *Bohemia*, vol. 18, no. 145 (2 December 1845), n.p., Fräul. Ržepka was a pupil at the Sophienakademie.

[3] Berlioz, *Mémoires*, vol. 2, p. 240. Anna Claudius sang one of Berlioz's songs at a soirée of pupils of the blind teacher Josef Proksch, according to *Bohemia*, vol. 19, no. 42 (5 April 1846), n.p. Proksch's *Musikbildungsanstalt* was at Altstädter Ring No. 603. I do not know whether Berlioz was present on that occasion, but he attended a subsequent soirée there

This, our penultimate chapter, is about Berlioz's last three weeks in Prague. Eduard Hanslick and August Wilhelm Ambros do not figure prominently at this stage of our narrative; the nobs had decided that Berlioz was safely lionizable, so the young student and the minor government official could be thrust aside except insofar as they were useful for the practical details of concert-giving. Besides, both must have fallen seriously behind in their obligations, Hanslick to his studies at the university and Ambros to the Ministry of Finance.

Berlioz returned to Prague on 25 March 1846 from his side-trips to Vienna, Budapest, and Breslau. On 31 March he conducted the concert already mentioned in which he performed for the first time in Prague the "Songe" of the *Symphonie fantastique*. On 7 April he conducted a concert in Prague for the benefit of a religious foundation; on 17 April he gave his sixth and final concert in Prague, the performance of his *Romeo and Juliet* Symphony to which he refers in the foregoing long quotation.

The two most important events to be described in this chapter are the formal dinner held in honour of Berlioz on 15 April, and his performance of *Romeo and Juliet* two days later. In his *Mémoires* Berlioz reverses the order of these two events, apparently for literary effect; I shall do the same. First, the concert.

Franz Liszt arrived in Prague from Brno on 9 April and put up at the Palais Platteis, where he also played his concerts. The first of these was on the 13th (Easter Monday); he played two more concerts on this visit, on the 16th and the 18th. In a letter Berlioz wrote on 16 April from Prague, we read that Liszt attended not only the performance of the *Romeo and Juliet* Symphony, but also the dress rehearsal; and that he acted as Berlioz's interpreter at both. This letter was written the day after the rehearsal and the day before the performance. The euphoric Berlioz wrote, in part:

---

at which eight of Proksch's pupils played a transcription by Franz Neumann of the *Roman Carnival* Overture for four pianos and sixteen hands. Berlioz came in the company of Ambros and Gutt, and signed Proksch's guest book with a cordial inscription. I am indebted to Dr. Jitka Ludvová for information concerning this visit. See Josef Proksch, ed. Rudolf Müller, *Biographisches Denkmal aus dessen Nachlaßpapieren errichtet* (Reichenberg: Published by the Author, 1874), pp. 108–9; Emingerová, "Hector Berlioz à Prague," pp. 183–84.

Fig. 18. Josef Proksch, Prague's beloved blind music teacher
His pupils regaled Berlioz with a performance of the *Roman Carnival* Overture arranged for
sixteen hands at four pianos (see p. 93, note 3).

I gave a splendid concert in Breslau and then hurried back here, where I was awaited and where I found that the Sophienakademie had worked up the choruses in *Romeo and Juliet* to perfection. I breathed easier when I heard them for the first time sung by amateur choristers, so unlike the caterwaulers in opera houses.[4] Yesterday we had our last full rehearsal; many people were allowed in, and Liszt helped by acting as my interpreter.

I had the pleasure of seeing him astonished and moved many times by this composition, which until then was totally unknown to him.... In the opinion of everyone here, as well as in Vienna, the Adagio is the best piece I have written to date. Yesterday, at the rehearsal, this piece and the "Fête chez Capulet" were applauded tremendously, contrary to the local custom, which precludes any kind of demonstration at rehearsals.[5]

Liszt and Berlioz had been friends since December 1830, in Paris, when Liszt attended the première performance of the *Symphonie fantastique*. Liszt's piano transcription of this work was no small token of admiration and friendship.[6] Nobody would have thought it untoward that in Prague Berlioz, with his friend the great Franz Liszt available to interpret for him, dispensed with young Hanslick's services in that capacity for the occasion. (I do not know whether or not Hanslick attended the dress rehearsal or the performance, but it is unlikely that he did not, since this was the most talked-about event of Berlioz's sojourn in Prague.)

While Berlioz was on his conducting tour to Vienna, Budapest, and Breslau, August Wilhelm Ambros in Prague had not been idle. He missed no opportunity to keep the name of Berlioz before the public. The following two unsigned notices in *Bohemia* were almost certainly written by Ambros:

We are pleased to advise our readers that Hector Berlioz, moved by the splendid reception he encountered in artistically sensitive Prague, is

---

[4] In his youth, Berlioz earned his living for a time as a "caterwauler" in a Parisian opera house. Berlioz, *Mémoires*, vol. 1, pp. 91–95.

[5] Berlioz, *Correspondance*, vol. 3, pp. 334–35.

[6] Berlioz, arr. Liszt (piano solo), *Grande symphonie fantastique*.

going to come back to us in order to bring before the public, by whose gratifying approval the inspired Master felt highly honoured, a few more of his most important compositions. Berlioz had committed himself to a benefit concert in Vienna on the first of the month, so he hurried off despite flooded roads and many inconveniences along the way. It does us Pragers great honour that the foreign Master is so eager to be well known to us, and that he considers us uniquely capable of understanding his rather daring works. At the moment we do not know for sure whether he will come to us before or after his trip to Budapest. As we hear it, Berlioz will perform in Prague his great symphony *Romeo and Juliet* (from which we already know the "Fête chez Capulet," the "Love Scene," and the "Queen Mab" scherzo), this time complete with the choral Finale. In addition, he may give another concert, including a few numbers from his celebrated *Requiem*, and his *Harold* Symphony.[7]

Berlioz's first concert in Budapest was held on 25 March and was a brilliant success. The following details are taken from a letter from Berlioz to Dr. Ambros. Nothing in his description is exaggerated, as anyone will agree who knows the unassuming Master personally. Any kind of direct compliment regarding his works greatly embarrasses him. Berlioz writes: "I gave my first concert here today, with the same result as in Prague. Four pieces were encored. I aroused the passions of the crowd with a Hungarian national tune, the 'Rákóczy March,' of which I had made an elaborate arrangement for orchestra. You cannot imagine the delirious ovation, the shouts of 'Bravo!' and the pounding of feet. . . ." In another letter, this one to Director Kittl, Berlioz promises to come back to Prague around 26 or 27 March. He says that it is his dearest wish to spend a few more days in the city in which the musicians and audiences displayed such flattering comprehension of his music. In this same letter he writes that he has recently made some major revisions to his symphony-cantata *Romeo and Juliet,* that he considers it his finest work, and, for the most part, worthy to be offered to performers and audiences in Prague.[8]

---

[7] [August Wilhelm Ambros?], [Unsigned notice], *Bohemia*, vol. 19, no. 17 (8 February 1846), n.p.

[8] [August Wilhelm Ambros?], [Unsigned notice], *Bohemia*, vol. 19, no. 23 (22 February 1846), n.p. This notice quotes accurately from Berlioz's letter to Ambros, but not so accurately from his letter to Kittl. For the former see Berlioz, *Correspondance*, vol. 3, pp. 316–17; for the latter p. 318.

Romeo and Juliet was performed, not in the Ständetheater, which had the advantage of a greater seating capacity, but in the Sophieninselsaal. In a letter to Ambros, Berlioz wrote: "This symphony cannot be performed in the Ständetheater the way it is."[9] We noticed in Chapter III that Berlioz considered the theatre "a dark, poky, and grubby place with a very bad sound"; but I think the main reason he chose the Sophieninselsaal was purely mechanical. In his "Remarks on the Performance" of *Romeo and Juliet,* Berlioz calls for a raised platform to be constructed over the orchestra pit, and ramps and other platforms on the stage, with the chorus of Capulets to the right, the Montagues to the left, the Prologue choristers somewhere else, and so on.[10] The performance was scheduled for 4:30 p.m. of 17 April; there was to be a performance that night at the Ständetheater, but not of an opera (as Berlioz says in the long quotation with which this chapter begins)—it was Schiller's *William Tell.* There would not have been time to strike Berlioz's elaborate construction and prepare the stage in time for the evening performance.

It may have been by coincidence that the Ständetheater, on 15 April, the day of Berlioz's dress rehearsal of the *Romeo and Juliet* Symphony, presented Bellini's opera on the Romeo and Juliet theme, *Montagues and Capulets.* I am sure that Berlioz made no secret of his lack of admiration for this opera,[11] and in *Ost und West* an anonymous reviewer, to be quoted in a moment, speaks harshly of it. Apart from routine reviews in the Prague journals, however, I have seen no mention of this particular performance. Berlioz, Hanslick, Ambros, and others who wrote about those weeks in "Berliozstadt" Prague are silent concerning it. This is one of the many striking gaps in our documentation. Was the performance scheduled for that date to honour Berlioz? To spite him? J.H. Hoffmann formally took over as director of the theatre earlier that week; the scheduling of Bellini's opera may have been the work of his predecessor, J.A. Stöger.

With his *Romeo and Juliet* Berlioz had taken an artistic step into the unknown, had forged a new genre, the so-called "dramatic symphony,"

---

[9] Berlioz, *Correspondance,* vol. 3, p. 322.
[10] Eulenburg pocket score, pp. vii–viii.
[11] Berlioz, *Mémoires,* vol. 1, pp. 214–16.

something between a conventional opera and a symphony. He was anxiously trying it out on the Pragers, having had no success with it in Vienna. To some people it must have seemed tactless, if not malicious, for the Ständetheater to mount in the same week a performance of an all-too-conventional opera on the same theme as that of Berlioz's dramatic symphony.

The choral and vocal solo parts in *Romeo and Juliet* were sung on this occasion in German, not in the original French. It must be difficult for a composer who has composed a dramatic work in his own language to perform it in another; Berlioz does not complain of this, however. No German version of the text was published until more than a decade later, but on his first German tour Berlioz had with him a German translation, and used it in Leipzig. [12] For the performance in Prague Berlioz made revisions, as we have already seen. These entailed alterations in the text; Berlioz asked Ambros to make the corresponding changes in the German, [13] presumably of the version used in Leipzig.

For an indication of how seriously the Pragers took Berlioz's claim to have created a new artistic genre, I here translate excerpts from the reviews of the *Romeo and Juliet* performance in *Bohemia* (Bernhard Gutt) and *Ost und West* (unsigned, but presumably Ambros). I begin with the latter.

> It was by introducing voices in the last movement of his Ninth Symphony that Beethoven stretched to breaking-point the limits of symphonic form, thereby giving notice that instrumental musical effects can be made to subordinate themselves to specific nonmusical ideas. Of this the singing in the Finale of the Ninth is all the proof we need.
>
> Subsequently the inspired genius Berlioz has, in his *Romeo and Juliet* Symphony, expanded the form still further and thereby established a totally new genre essentially distinct from oratorio, cantata, and symphony.
>
> We confess that we went to hear this work with misgivings, and expected some kind of musical hybrid monstrosity, but our prejudice

---

[12] The German translation was made in Paris by Professor Duesberg. Berlioz, *Mémoires*, vol. 2, pp. 92–93.

[13] Berlioz, *Correspondance*, vol. 3, pp. 313, 318, 322.

was totally overcome and we have to acknowledge this as altogether a well-organized masterwork. The Prague audience was of the same opinion, since the applause was never so enthusiastic at performances of works by Berlioz as on this occasion, so tumultuous and prolonged. The composer was recalled several times after each piece. Now we have the measure of the Viennese critics and their judgements. From now on we shall pay not the slightest attention to critical pronouncements from Vienna!

The composer's choice of subject was very felicitous, since this Shakespearean love-tragedy, an imperishable masterwork, contains much more in the way of musical features than in the way of plot. This is why Bellini, in his operatic version, considered himself obliged to make a heroic character of Romeo, which he then absurdly contradicted and made into a piece of self-mockery by assigning the part to a female voice. It bespeaks a curious reverence for Italian opera that people still sit through this ridiculous botch.

Conflict (two hostile families) and eventual reconciliation (at the graveside of the lovers): that is the basic idea running through the whole work, and it is carefully brought out by Berlioz. It is an idea based upon the nature of music itself; but language has taken from music such expressions of its own as "dissonance," "unison," "harmony," and then applied them to *all* the arts. The intervening themes (the rapture of love, festiveness, humour), the treatment of which the Romantic poets brought to the greatest heights, are in turn especially suited to being rendered in music.[14]

The author of these philosophically interesting remarks found the Adagio (the scene in Capulet's garden) prolix, but otherwise thought he might come to prefer *Romeo and Juliet* over all other works by Berlioz.

Following this review in *Ost und West* is a brief report of the banquet held on 15 April in honour of Berlioz, ending with a little journalistic scoop: "We have just learned that Herr Berlioz has it in mind to visit Prague again next year, and put on his new dramatic symphony *Faust* for the Pragers first, rather than for the Parisians." As we know, this did not happen, but it would have been a delicious piece of one-upmanship for Prague over Paris if it had.

---

[14] [August Wilhelm Ambros?], [Unsigned notice], *Ost und West*, vol. 10, no. 47 (21 April 1846), pp. 187–88. Berlioz *Mémoires*, vol. 1, p. 214: "Quel sujet! Comme tout est dessiné pour la musique!"

Here are excerpts from Bernhard Gutt's review of *Romeo and Juliet* in *Bohemia*:

Prague has appreciated Hector Berlioz perhaps the most warmly of all German cities. With a performance of his dramatic symphony *Romeo and Juliet* (for orchestra with choir, vocal solos and recitative) he has made a worthy farewell to our city. . . . Prague will hold him in affectionate memory, as he will Prague. . . .[15]

The work is an immediate continuation of the direction Berlioz took in his *Symphony fantastique*. Indeed, the dramatic symphony carries passion, ever more deeply stirred, further to an externalization, to the actuality of situations. In the *Symphony fantastique* the tone-poet himself stood in the midst of the dramatic action; the feelings he objectified in any given situation were his own. The advantages and disadvantages of this crucial step are obvious. Even if definiteness of expression is thereby assured without need of further commentary . . . along with diversity and intensification of feeling, the musical work will be in danger of abandoning its *raison d'être* [*Selbstgeltung*] altogether. One must admit that the loss is greater than the gain. The best thing, then, is always to put up with the loss and take advantage of the gain as best one can. I had expected Berlioz to put the culmination of the drama before us in more realistic fashion,[16] and to presuppose that we are familiar with Shakespeare's poem, which is part of the heritage of all educated people;[17] but, since the text was written according to his instructions and with his participation, he inserts himself into the action of the drama, which, however, he cannot then present intact. This very

---

[15] Bernhard Gutt [here "B.G."], "Drittes und letztes Concert des Herrn Hector Berlioz," *Bohemia*, vol. 19, no. 50 (19 April 1846), n.p. In our text the excerpt immediately following is from the continuation of Gutt's article in the succeeding issue. It is fully cited in note 19 below.

[16] In the *Romeo and Juliet* Symphony we neither see nor hear the deaths of Romeo and Juliet in the tomb; indeed, the only character from Shakespeare's play who puts in an appearance in Berlioz's dramatic symphony is Friar Laurence, not to utter any of the lines Shakespeare wrote for him, but to sing an exhortation to the mourning families at the end.

[17] Gutt has nothing to say in favour of Berlioz's Prologue to the *Romeo and Juliet* Symphony. Here he complains that the only purpose the Prologue serves is to tell us what we already know about Shakespeare's *Romeo and Juliet*.

fragmentary narrative is assigned to a recitatival Prologue, which by nature is unsusceptible to musical treatment. So paltry a makeshift is uncalled for. Since Beethoven, people have written music of the most specific coloration, of truly dramatic power of expression, to well-known poetical works, especially dramas. Nobody took exception to this, since it was an after-effect of the feeling aroused by the poetry itself upon the purely musical domain. With the most important situations in the Shakespearean tragedy, Berlioz could undertake something similar with every justification; also when he has persons and groups of people speaking directly by means of song. But his Prologue is nothing but program notes set to music. What might he say to the suggestion that he have the relevant passages from his printed program notes to the *Symphonie fantastique* sung in recitative before each movement?

The *Romeo and Juliet* Symphony has been called something midway between the symphony and the secular oratorio, a newly devised genre. A symphony that followed the emotional situations of a given drama in its sequence of movements, even if it rose to the immediacy of song, would abandon its proper ground, but in individuality of expression it would take on all the more powerful an effectiveness thereby; on the other hand, a secular oratorio would be in as untenable a position as a drama that forsook the stage; it would be a disembodied, chimerical opera.[18] A species lying between these two aberrations would be totally self-destructive.

Berlioz continues to move in the direction of the dramatic symphony; he is currently at work on a musical transformation of Goethe's *Faust*, which perhaps we shall hear under his own direction during the coming year. We may confidently predict that this composition will have in it many things of great beauty. Nevertheless, it is my opinion that the "dramatic symphony" as a genre has no future.[19]

---

[18] Gutt is here taking a preliminary swing at Robert Schumann's secular oratorio *Das Paradies und die Peri*, which had its first Prague performance the following month. Gutt's point is that the expression "secular oratorio" is self-contradictory. Eduard "Hanslik" commemorated the abovementioned performance with an extravaganza, "Robert Schumann und seine Cantate 'Das Paradies und die Peri': Ein Brief an Flamin, den letzten Davidsbündler," *Ost und West,* vol. 10, no. 59 (19 May 1846), pp. 235–36.

[19] Bernhard Gutt [here "B.G."], "Die dramatische Symphonie des Hector Berlioz," *Bohemia,* vol. 19, no. 51 (21 April 1846), n.p. This is a continuation of Gutt's review begun in the preceding issue.

"The dramatic symphony is an ill-fated hybrid with no future." So wrote the mature Eduard Hanslick in 1863 concerning a performance in Vienna of Berlioz's *Romeo and Juliet* Symphony.[20] This review has so much in common with Gutt's of 1846 that it could be charitably regarded as Hanslick's unconscious recollection of the latter. Hanslick has left nothing on record concerning the performance in Prague of this work; it is tempting to suppose that he attended it (he must have been back in the city from his Easter vacation in Vienna by that time), and that he was undergoing a crisis in his own thinking about Berlioz and about music in general. When Hanslick wrote "Ritter Berlioz in Prague" a few weeks earlier, he was in no doubt that it is possible for composers to make poetry in musical sounds, that it is aesthetically acceptable for music to be regarded as subservient to the requirements of literary texts. This was the prevailing view of the matter. But Bernhard Gutt in his review attacked it head on; the anonymous reviewer in *Ost und West* challenged it obliquely; Hanslick a few months later, and for the rest of his life, rejected it altogether. We return to this in our final chapter.

It remains here to tell of the banquet in honour of Hector Berlioz. It was held in the Hotel Three Lindens on the evening of 15 April 1846. It was the Pragers' adieu to the Bow Wow, the Mumbo Jumbo, the (formerly) Great Unknown. Here is *Bohemia*'s account of the event, written presumably by August Wilhelm Ambros:

> A number of admirers of the inspired artist Hector Berlioz got together to present a banquet in honour of this famous composer prior to his departure from Prague. . . . The company, which had gathered to demonstrate to the guest of honour the high esteem he had won in musical Prague through his compositions, consisted of men of the upper levels of the aristocracy, and of artists, particularly of musicians (in keeping with the purpose of the evening).
>
> A portrait of Berlioz, placed under a laurel wreath, marked the place of honour. Following the meal, which enlivened an informal conversation, the toasts were proposed, not with prepared speeches full of pretentious verbosity, but with a few sincere words spoken on the spur of the moment. The first toast was to the celebrated guest of honour,

---

[20] Hanslick, *Concertsaal*, p. 290.

and the succeeding ones were to the others present, all men of distinction: Liszt, Dreyschock,[21] Prince Camille de Rohan,[22] Count Thun,[23] Director Kittl, Veit,[24] Franz Škroup, Strakaty, Director Ruben,[25] among many others. There were, in addition, three cheers for Bohemia and for Prague. In conclusion, Liszt, like Berlioz a true artist in every fibre of his being, and as charming and brilliant, presented Berlioz with a commemorative silver chalice; his glowing testimonial address was fraught with the significance of higher inspiration, full of pith and vitality. He referred to the way Berlioz, "ce cratère de génie," had struggled for recognition against unspeakable obstacles, with firm resolve; how, paying no heed to the scorn of bigots and the slander of desiccated journeymen in the art of music, Berlioz kept on in pursuit of his clearly perceived artistic goal until he achieved it. The audience (said Liszt) for which Mozart wrote his *Don Giovanni* could not fail to appreciate Berlioz. (And, truly, Liszt is right about that.) The very distinguished members of the gathering showed their approval throughout Liszt's presentation, mainly by means of the enthusiastic cheers with which they received his heartfelt words.

This splendid evening demonstrated to Berlioz just how much Prague understands him, loves and admires him.[26]

---

[21] Alexander Dreyschock (1818–1869), pupil of Tomaschek, virtuoso pianist, composer of piano pieces. Berlioz knew him well and admired him.

[22] Camille-Philippe-Joseph-Idesbald, Prince de Rohan-Guéménée, Rochefort et Montauban, Duc de Bouillon et Montbazon (1801–1892). For all that, see Berlioz, *Correspondance*, vol. 3, p. 335n. Prince Rohan was a naturalized Austrian citizen living in Prague. For an amusing vignette of him at the age of eighty taking the cure at Karlsbad, see Hanslick, *Leben*, vol. 2, pp. 210–11.

[23] Graf Leo Thun-Hohenstein (1811–1888), a leading political figure of the Prague Vormärz and the revolutionary year 1848; friend of Hanka, Palacký and other Czech nationalists.

[24] Presumably Wenzel Heinrich Veit (1806–1864), magistrate and composer. Veit composed "Episode in the Life of a Tailor," a parody of Berlioz's *Symphonie fantastique*.

[25] Christian Ruben (1805–1875), a famous historical painter, was Director of the Imperial Academy of Fine Arts in Prague at the time of Berlioz's visit. Later he held the corresponding position in Vienna.

[26] [August Wilhelm Ambros?], [Unsigned notice], *Bohemia*, vol. 19, no. 49 (17 April 1846), n.p.

To conclude our narrative, but not our book, here is Berlioz's version of the banquet:

> You will recall that I told you about the banquet held in my honour by the musicians and music-lovers of Vienna, at which they presented me with a silver baton. Not to be outdone, the Pragers held something similar . . . at which they presented me with a silver cup. Most of the local musicians, critics, and patrons turned up. I had the pleasure of seeing amongst the latter a compatriot, the witty and genial Prince de Rohan. By unanimous consent, Liszt was appointed Master of Ceremonies in place of the President, who was not sufficiently versed in the French language. At the first toast, Liszt delivered to me, on behalf of all those present, an oration lasting at least a quarter of an hour; his words displayed a warmth of spirit, and abundance of ideas and a felicity of expression which professional orators might well have envied. I was deeply touched.
>
> Unfortunately, Liszt drank as fervently as he spoke: that perfidious cup launched the participants upon such a flood of champagne as shipwrecked all the eloquence of Liszt. At two o'clock in the morning, on the streets of Prague, it took all the persuasive powers of Belloni [Liszt's manager] and myself to get him to wait until daylight to fight a duel (he was absolutely bent on it) with pistols at two paces with a Bohemian who had drunk ever better than he. At dawn we were not without concern for Liszt, who had to play a concert at noon that day. At half past eleven he was still asleep. Upon awakening at last, he got into a diligence, arrived at the concert hall, received a tremendous ovation as he came on stage, and played, I believe, as he never before played in his life.[27]
>
> There's a special God who looks after pianists.
>
> Adieu, my dear Ferrand. I fear you will have no occasion to complain that my letters are laconic. Yet I have by no means said all I would like to say about my fond regrets at having left Prague and its inhabitants. As you know, I have a deep passion for music. From that you can judge

---

[27] As usual, Berlioz is striving for literary effect. Whatever the literal truth of the other details, there can have been no question of loading poor Liszt into a diligence to take him to his recital. Liszt performed in the Platteissaal and stayed at the Palais Platteis, all surrounding a single courtyard. In a few minutes he could have walked comfortably from his bed to the concert platform without stepping outdoors.

for yourself how much I love the Bohemians. O Praga! quando te aspiciam! [O Prague! when shall I see you again?][28]

He never did.

---

[28] Berlioz, *Mémoires*, vol. 2, p. 243. David Cairns points out that the Latin words are a paraphrase of Horace, *Satires*, II, vi: "O rus, quando ego te aspiciam" ("O country home, when shall I see you again?"). Hector Berlioz, trans. and ed. David Cairns, *The Memoirs of Hector Berlioz* . . . (London: Victor Gollancz, 1969), p. 412.

VIII
Volte-face: Eduard Hanslick and Bernhard Gutt

WHEN IN 1846 Hector Berlioz introduced himself to us with a series of brilliant concerts, his music blazed forth like a meteor. It was so undreamed of, so dazzling, so utterly unlike all that was considered fit and proper, that it overpowered the astonished listeners, eliciting boundless admiration from some and mortal hatred from others. Nobody remained uninvolved, nobody was neutral. Only an extraordinary personality could have had such an effect; a Frenchman who wrote symphonies and worshipped Beethoven and Shakespeare as his gods was already something altogether extraordinary. Also, the hallmark of a significant artistic event was not lacking: that it provides an occasion to raise questions of musical form and content, of the limits of music's territory, of its relation to poetry and painting—all these were stirred up by Berlioz's music. The inherited laws of aesthetics were scrutinized and put to the test.[1]

One outcome of the controversy Hanslick describes here was his conversion to the view expressed by Bernhard Gutt in his *King Lear* review of 1845, namely that this overture is not music. In his 1846 essay on Berlioz, Gutt wrote:

> Berlioz's is not a musical but a poetical kind of creative activity. Instead of composing music, he wants to make poetry out of musical elements.[2]

An essay published in Vienna fifteen months later showed that Hanslick had by then adopted Gutt's view of the matter. Gone forever was his youthful enthusiasm for the tone-poet of the *Symphonie fantastique*, for the tone-painter of the "Pilgrims' March." Hanslick wrote:

---

[1] Eduard Hanslick, *Suite: Aufsätze über Musik und Musiker* (Vienna and Teschen: Prochaska, n.d.), pp. 95–96. This volume contains selections from Hanslick's writings of 1872–82.
[2] Gutt [here "B.G."], "Hector Berlioz," n.p.

> The distinguishing characteristic of Berlioz is that for him music is not autonomous, not music in the strict sense . . . but a means of expression for the representation of a poetic conception. B. Gutt rightly says that Berlioz does not compose music, but creates poetry out of musical elements.[3]

This was a true *volte-face* on Hanslick's part and not an aberration, since he adhered to his new position, and its theoretical implications, for the rest of his life.

So far is I am aware, Hanslick mentions Gutt only twice in his writings; the second occasion stands above. The first is Hanslick's remark in "Ritter Berlioz in Prague" in which he hints that "the redoubtable B. Gutt" had not adequately studied the score of the *King Lear* Overture and for this reason made his ridiculous assertion that this overture is not music.

Hanslick left no confessions, no metaphysical journal, so we cannot trace the stages of his transition from one aesthetical view to its opposite. Certainly questions about fundamental artistic principles were raised in response to Berlioz's concerts in Prague; Hanslick could hardly have kept out of the debate, although apart from "Ritter Berlioz in Prague" he contributed nothing to it in print. No doubt he and Berlioz discussed such matters together, but of this there is no record. Berlioz must have been aware to some extent of the Pragers' earnest, characteristically Germanic disputations about his music and about the nature of music in general, and may have been amused by them.

Could there have been some kind of rift between Berlioz and Hanslick that might account for the latter's second thoughts about the former's music? The answer must be negative if we may judge by some of the fragments from Berlioz's correspondence quoted in Chapter VI above.

The year 1846 was a time of sustained and extreme intellectual stimulation for Hanslick, then in his early twenties—an age at which sensitive people are most vulnerable to such impressions as he then received in profusion. In addition to his excitement over Berlioz in January, March, and April, there was Hanslick's Easter vacation in Vienna. There he met Franz Liszt and the violin virtuoso Heinrich

---

[3] Hanslick, "Becher," p. 123.

Wilhelm Ernst, to whom he had letters of introduction from Berlioz; he also met a famous Bohemian composer named Adalbert Gyrowetz, a man of great age and distinction who had been a colleague and personal friend of Haydn, Mozart, and Beethoven (Gyrowetz was a pallbearer at Beethoven's funeral); he met poets, painters, journalists, and yet more musicians; he attended plays and concerts. Although he reported that Vienna had nothing to compare with the Roßmarkt or the Karlsbrücke, he was in a state of euphoria most of his time there.[4]

Then on 19 May 1846, in *Ost und West*, Hanslick's "Robert Schumann and his Cantata *Das Paradies und die Peri*: a Letter to Flamin, the Last of the Davidsbündler" appeared.[5] Although this writing is referred to in the literature on Hanslick as a review, it contains little musical criticism. It is mainly prattle, an elaborate in-joke addressed to the Davids in Prague. Hanslick dispatched a copy of it in haste to Schumann in Leipzig, who then invited the young author to visit him and Clara that summer in Dresden. Hanslick accepted, and also arranged to visit Wagner there (Hanslick first met Wagner the previous year at Marienbad). In Dresden he heard Wagner conducting *Tannhäuser*; this in turn led to Hanslick's remarkable essay on that opera in eleven instalments in the *Wiener Allgemeine Musik-Zeitung* during the last weeks of 1846.[6] Hanslick dispatched a copy of this essay in haste to Wagner in Dresden, who, on New Year's Day 1847, wrote a long letter to the young critic in acknowledgement; but this letter belongs to another documentary narrative.

Throughout all this intellectual and artistic excitement Hanslick had the benefit of the steadying influence of two philosophical scholars who

---

[4] Hanslick, *Leben*, vol. 1, pp. 79–92.

[5] Hanslick [here "Hanslik"], "Robert Schumann," pp. 235–36.

[6] Eduard Hanslick [here "Eduard Hanslik"], "Richard Wagner, und seine neueste Oper 'Tannhäuser': Eine Beurtheilung," *Wiener Allgemeine Musik-Zeitung*, vol. 6, no. 143 (28 November 1846), p. 581; no. 144 (1 December 1846), p. 585; no. 145 (3 December 1846), pp. 589–90; no. 148 (10 December 1846), pp. 601–2; no. 149 (12 December 1846), pp. 605–6; no. 150 (15 December 1846), pp. 613–14, no. 151 (17 December 1846), pp. 617–18; no. 152 (19 December 1846), p. 621; no. 153 (22 December 1846), pp. 625–26; nos. 154 and 155 (24 and 26 December 1846), pp. 629–30; no. 156 (29 December 1846), pp. 637–38. Not only is this essay exceptionally long for this journal, but most instalments begin on the first page. This is remarkable treatment for an unknown author from the provinces, barely twenty-one years old.

were, like himself, especially interested in aesthetical matters: his friend Robert Zimmermann, and his father, J.A. Hanslik. It is perhaps due largely to their influence that Eduard emerged from this critical period in his life capable of articulating the new aesthetical position he had adopted, a position to which he first gave expression in print in his essay "Dr. Alfred Julius Becher" in April 1847, as quoted above, p. 108. It is a classical and formalistic position directly opposed to the *Enthusiasmus* of the Davids that he had earlier expressed in his "Ritter Berlioz in Prague." My personal belief is that the single most important factor in Hanslick's change of view was the influence of the journalist Bernhard Gutt, to whom we must now turn for a closer look.[7]

Gutt was born in Potsdam in 1812 and died in Prague of apoplexy in 1849. He studied medicine in Prague, but never practised. As we know, he was for some years co-editor of *Bohemia* (he also held a similar position with *Deutsche Zeitung aus Böhmen*). He wrote short stories which appeared in print, and a tragedy which did not; the latter was never performed, but he was held in highest regard for his critical writings on theatre and music in Prague. His early death (at the age of thirty-seven) was generally considered to be due to alcoholism, the effects of which are evident in the writings of his last few months.

I have encountered no indication that Gutt and Hanslick were friends, although they must have been acquaintances, since as reviewers they attended many of the same performances in Prague. Hanslick was still legally a minor in 1846; perhaps his parents had reservations about his associating with a man whose alcoholism must by then have been evident and a matter of public knowledge.[8]

---

[7] For a more fully documented account of Bernhard Gutt and his influence on Hanslick see Geoffrey Payzant, "Eduard Hanslick and Bernhard Gutt," *The Music Review*, vol. 50, no. 2 (May 1989) [appeared in October 1990], pp. 124–33.

Documentation regarding Gutt is scarce. My account is based on the following sources: Wurzbach, *Biographisches Lexikon*, s.v. "Gutt, Bernhard"; [A. Schmidt and B.F. Voigt, eds.], *Neuer Nekrolog der Deutschen*, vol. 27 (1849), item 74 "Bernhard Gutt" (Weimar: Voigt, 1851); Oscar Teuber, *Geschichte des Prager Theaters: Von den Anfängen des Schauspielwesens bis auf die neueste Zeit*, 3 vols. (Prague: Haase, 1888), vol. 3, pp. 285–86; Jan Wenig, *Sie waren in Prag* (Prague: Editio Supraphon, 1971), pp. 83–103.

[8] Hanslick tells us that he had a very sheltered (*häuslich*) upbringing, and that he never visited a coffee house in Prague; so it is possible that he and Gutt never conversed (Hanslick, *Leben*, vol. 1, p. 93).

Not long after Gutt's death on 25 March 1849 an essay by August Wilhelm Ambros with the title "Bernhard Gutt as Musician" appeared in *Bohemia* in three instalments. In it Ambros states his opinion that Gutt was capable of writing a full-scale aesthetics of music, but that he was forced by circumstances to squander his immense intellectual capital in dribs and drabs in the form of reviews to be read today and forgotten tomorrow.[9] Having examined Gutt's music criticisms in *Bohemia*, particularly those written in response to the Berlioz concerts in Prague, I have to agree with Ambros that a coherent musical aesthetics lurks among them. I dare go further and state that it surfaced five years later, entirely unacknowledged, in the first edition of Eduard Hanslick's *Vom Musikalisch-Schönen*.

To show the full extent of Hanslick's debt to Gutt would require a line-by-line commentary on that book. Here I shall have to be content with a few of the more pertinent examples.

The first is a comparison of a passage from Gutt's essay on Berlioz (1846) with one from Hanslick's "Becher" essay (1847) and another from his *On the Musically Beautiful* (1854).

Gutt in 1846:

> Each of Berlioz's works . . . appears to be a translation of a poem into tones. . . . Because it is impossible to render anything definite in series and combinations of tones, any music of which this is nevertheless expected requires a guidebook for the listener, a retranslation of the music back into the words out of which it was created in the first place. The detailed program of the *Symphonie fantastique* was not intended as a mere nudge to the audience . . . it was a necessity.[10]

Hanslick in 1847:

> Because of music's inability to reproduce anything concrete in tonal combinations, Berlioz's music, which nevertheless strives to do this, requires a guidebook for the listener, a retranslation of the music back

---

[9] Ambros [here "A.W. Ambros"], "Bernhard Gutt als Musiker," *Bohemia*, vol. 22, no. 78 (1 April 1849), n.p. The remaining two instalments appeared in vol. 22, no. 79 (2 April 1849) and no. 81 (5 April 1849).

[10] Gutt [here "B.G."], "Berlioz" (27 January 1846), n.p.

into words. For this reason, all of Berlioz's compositions have programs and translations, and *must* have them.[11]

Hanslick in 1854:

> The composer of a piece of instrumental music does not have in mind the representation of a specific content. If he does this . . . [h]is composition becomes the translation of a program into tones which are then unintelligible without the program. We neither deny nor underestimate the conspicuous talent of Berlioz if we mention his name here.[12]

Our second example comes close to plagiarism by the standards of the twentieth century, although it would have been less objectionable in the 1850s when Hanslick wrote it. Gutt had been safely dead for five years by then, so there was little danger that any but a few close friends from Prague would notice the cribbing.

Some background to the example may be helpful. The excitement in Prague over Berlioz was at its height when, on 6 April 1846, *Moses*—an oratorio by the German composer and theorist Adolph Bernhard Marx—was performed there. Bernhard Gutt reviewed the performance in *Bohemia* of 9 April and also wrote an essay on *Moses* itself; this essay appeared in three instalments, 10, 11, and 14 April. It contains several extended passages more philosophical than journalistic in character, as did Gutt's essay on Berlioz earlier the same year. Berlioz was in Prague at the time of the performance, but there is no evidence that he attended it. Hanslick missed it, since he was in Vienna at the time, but he very obviously did not miss Gutt's essay in *Bohemia*. In the first instalment of his essay on Marx, Gutt wrote:

> The essence of musical form is rhythm: rhythm in the large, namely the eurhythmy of a beautifully articulated structure; and rhythm in the small, namely the regular beat of individual units within the metric period.[13]

---

[11] Hanslick, "Becher," p. 123.

[12] Hanslick, *Musically Beautiful*, p. 35.

[13] "Das Wesen der musikalischen Form ist der Rhythmus, der Rhythmus im Großen, nämlich die Eurhythmie eines schön gegliedertes Baues, der Rhythmus im Kleinen, die

Eight years later, in *On the Musically Beautiful*, the following words appeared under Hanslick's name:

> [The essence of music] is rhythm: rhythm in the large as the co-proportionality of a symmetrical structure; and rhythm in the small as regular alternating motion of individual units within the metric period.[14]

For some further examples I shall simply quote a few lines from Gutt's 1846 essay on Berlioz; in these lines, readers who are familiar with Hanslick's *On the Musically Beautiful* will recognize ideas and phrases which are basic to his argument in that book, and elaborated by him in it.

> Musical expression is ambiguous, not explicit; hence the many attempts to define and determine it with words and metaphors. These attempts invariably fail, because the subjectivity of musical language is directly opposed to the immutability of the poetical, as is the indefiniteness of feeling to the definiteness of words. The true beauty of a musical artwork can be neither described nor proven; hence, to every musically cultivated person it is immediately and totally accessible,

gesetzmäßige Schwebung der einzelnen Glieder im Zeitmaße." Bernhard Gutt [here "B.G."], "Mose, Oratorium von Dr. Adolph Bernhard Marx," *Bohemia*, vol. 19, no. 45 (10 April 1846), n.p. In architectural literature, a structure (typically a Greek or Roman temple) is said to possess eurhythmy to the extent that its observable dimensions, and those of its substructural components, are mathematically proportional to one another, the ultimate determinants of their relationships being numerical. By analogy, a musical composition may be regarded as a complex structure whose features are likewise co-proportional, the ultimate determinants of their relationships being the physical and psychological properties of the diatonic system.

[14] "Das Urelement der Musik ist Wohllaut, ihr Wesen Rhythmus. Rhythmus im großen, als die Uebereinstimmung eines symmetrischen Baues, und Rhythmus im kleinen, als die wechselnd-gesetzmäßige Bewegung einselner Glieder im Zeitmaß." Hanslick, *Vom Musikalisch-Schönen*, p. 32. For Gutt's Germanized Greek word "Eurhythmie" Hanslick substitutes the German "Uebereinstimmung", which I translate "co-proportionality" in the passage here cited and in Hanslick, *Musically Beautiful*, p. 28. The three words may here be regarded as synonymous. Carl Dalhaus, in an essay on this very passage, supposes that it originated with Hanslick; he does not mention Bernhard Gutt. Carl Dahlhaus, "Rhythmus im Großen," *MELOS/NZ*, vol. 1, no. 3 (June 1975), pp. 439–41.

incapable of being misinterpreted. It is nothing but the immediate manifestation of the musical idea. . . .

It is difficult to talk about all that without bogging down in pedantry. Let us look at the creative act of the composer. The composer works from the centre of the musical idea toward the circumference of the tonal structure. . . .

All admirers of [Berlioz's] compositions find in them not so much a self-contained collocation of musical sensations as a poetical sequence of masterfully expressed images and ideas. One can never interpret real music in such manner without imposing extreme coercion upon it, indeed, without destroying it. Nevertheless we always have to resort to metaphors and subjective analogies for describing musical impressions; but it can never be the purpose of music to induce in us directly the abovementioned sequences of images and ideas. It is, moreover, impossible to explain how it is that one and the same composition can be interpreted visually or poetically in entirely different ways, as often happens.[15]

*　　*　　*　　*　　*

Eduard Hanslick is not the only figure in our narrative who had second thoughts about the music of Berlioz; Robert Schumann is another, as we shall see in a moment; Ambros and Griepenkerl are two more. Ambros, in later life, took the view that this music belonged too much to its own time to have appeal for subsequent generations,[16] a judgement which Berlioz would have found ironic, since in his own time his music received little acceptance in his homeland.

In his autobiography, Hanslick concludes his account of Berlioz's triumphs in Prague with a description of the composer as he seemed fourteen years after, when Hanslick visited him in Paris.

That sturdy upright figure, that regal head with the eyes of an eagle, I found greatly changed. If I had run into him somewhere other than his out-of-the-way lodgings, I would have been hard put to recognize him.

---

[15] Gutt [here "B.G."], "Berlioz" (27 January 1846), n.p.
[16] Ambros, *Bunte Blätter*, pp. 93ff.

Indeed, the pallor of his sunken face and the totally whitened hair set off his delicately modelled features even more vividly, but the old strength and freshness had faded away. The eyes were dull and sickly, recalling the old fire only in occasional glances. A voluminous score lay open before him. I asked what he was working on. "Je suis occupé à souffrir" was the pathetic reply. Hand in hand with his physical suffering went a profound depression and a growing bitterness and isolation. The Parisians had regard only for his brilliant work as a critic; the composer Berlioz was ignored and ridiculed. He would have to go to Germany if he wanted to hear his compositions performed, he said. Those days in Prague and Vienna seemed to him like a golden dream.[17]

To conclude on a wry but less lugubrious note, here are a few lines from a long essay on Berlioz by Hanslick published in 1882:

Robert Schumann, who with his enthusiastic critique of the *Symphonie fantastique* was the first and most influential person in Germany to pledge allegiance to Berlioz's flag, tended in later years to speak of his erstwhile favourite very coldly, almost with distaste. I can still see the naughty grin with which Schumann, some thirty years ago, said to me: "You Pragers went right out of your minds over Berlioz, didn't you?" I permitted myself to respond in kind to his raillery with the question: "Yes, but who started it all?"[18]

---

[17] Hanslick, *Leben*, vol. 1, pp. 60–61. Hanslick mentions his 1860 sojourn in Paris in vol. 2, p. 48 and his last visit to Berlioz (1867) in vol. 2, pp. 63–64.
[18] Hanslick, *Suite*, p. 98. The essay from which I quote here has the title "Hector Berlioz in seinen Briefen und Memoiren." It appeared previously under that same title in *Deutsche Rundschau*, vol. 30 (January, February, March 1882), pp. 369–85. The little story about Hanslick's exchange with Schumann concerning Berlioz appears on p. 385.

Appendix

Ritter Berlioz in Prag.

„No, they cannot touch me for coining,
I am the king himself."
(*King Lear.*)

So eben komme ich aus Hektor Berlioz' erster Akademie. Es drängt mich den Zusammenklang der empfangenen Eindrücke, das Resultat meiner Studien and Gedanken über den Tondichter an die Spitze meines Berichtes zu stellen: Berlioz ist seit Beethoven die großartigste Erscheinung im Gebiet der musikalischen Dichtung. Hier gilt kein ängstliches Drehen und Winden, keine bedächtig-umschweifende Phrasenmacherei. Berlioz ist in der musikalischen Kritik Parteifrage geworden, hier heißt es: »Welf oder Ghibellin?« Ich habe meine Parole gegeben und wiederhole sie frei und freudigst. Der Mann, den man erst ignorirt, dann verlacht und verspottet, endlich verunglimpft und angefeindet hat: er ist ein gewaltiger Geist und ein großer Dichter!

Der geneigte Leser fürchte nicht, daß ich dieses Urtheil etwa in der Aufregung des Enthusiasmus, noch überwältigt von der Macht der eben empfangenen Eindrücke niedergeschrieben; man hat meinen Musik-Berichten, so mangelhaft sie sein mögen, nie den Vorwurf der Ueberschwänglichkeit machen können, und möge es auch diesmal nicht. Ich habe Berlioz' Kompositionen, so weit sie uns zugänglich sind, lange früher gekannt, und die am 19. d.M. aufgeführten zu wiederholten Malen gehört; mit jedem Male wuchs mein Verständniß und mit ihm meine Bewunderung. Zur Begründung meines Urtheils will ich vor Allem die wichtigsten Einwendungen, die bisher gegen die Zulässigkeit der Berlioz'schen Kompositionen erhoben wurden, aufführen und zu entkräften versuchen. Der Haupteinwurf, unter den man fast alle die speziellen Tadel subsummieren kann, lautet: »Wie kommt es, daß B.'s Werke, wenn ihnen der Geist und die Poesie wirklich inwohnt, die Ihr ihnen vindizirt, erstens das große Publikum nicht ansprechen, und zweitens auch von den Kritikern verworfen werden?[«]

Hinsichtlich des ersten Punktes kann ich nur mit Bedauern antworten, daß, seit die Musikwissenschaft in Theorie und Produktion immer oberflächlicher

---

Transcribed from *Ost und West*, 22 January 1848, pp. 35–36 and 24 January 1848, pp. 38–40, the copy in the Austrian National Library, Vienna, catalogue number 104.634-C. The *Fraktur* of the original appears here as roman type; roman type in the original is here in italics; letter-spaced words in the original are also expanded here.

betrieben wird, und seit in den letzten Perioden einerseits der Geschmack des
großen Publikums, andrerseits das Ideal der wahren Kunst immer weiter von
einander divergiren, das Urtheil des Publikums aufgehört hat, Kriterion für den
W e r t h eines Tonwerks zu sein. In der Musik ist nun einmal nicht Alles für Alle.
Es gehören Kenntnisse, es gehört eine lange Vertrautheit mit der Musik dazu, um
ein komplizirtes Tonstück in Geist und Form aufzufassen, und wer Fremdling in
der musikalischen Literatur ist, wird beim Anhören eines neuen Genres über
einige scharfe Ecken stolpern, und über ungewohnte Formen die Fassung
verlieren. Die große Mehrzahl ist nicht im Stande ein Tonwerk größerer
Dimensionen und überwiegend geistigen Elements zu v e r s t e h e n ; und ohne
Verständniß — kein Genuß. Das Ideal eines Kunstwerks, das durch Vereinigung
beider Faktoren der Schönheit (des Geistigen nämlich, und des Sinnlich-
reizenden) den Kenner und den Laien gleichmäßig befriedigt, ist gewiß nicht
unerreichbar; doch wird in unserer Zeit der Künstler gewiß schon auf der Einen
oder der Anderen Seite zu viel nachgeben müssen. Es ist thöricht, es dem großen
Publikum zum V o r w u r f zu machen, daß es die »Somnambula« dem »Paulus«
vorzieht; dies resultirt nothwendig aus dem Wesen der Tonkunst und ihrem
Verhältniß zur allgemeinen ästhetischen Ausbildung. Ich will es beileibe nicht
als nothwendig vertheidigen, daß die Mehrzahl am Schlechten Gefallen finde,
wohl aber daß eine gewisse Klasse des Musikalisch-Schönen, — und hierher
gehören eben die höchsten Bestrebungen — ihr immer unzugänglich bleibt.
Weit besser sind die bildenden Künste daran: sie darstellen stets ein Sichtbares,
Vorhandenes, Wirkliches; und das Wirkliche ist verständlich. Die Dichtkunst
hingegen hat, in ihren höheren Gattungen, mit der Musik den esoterischen
Charakter gemein; nur steht sie insofern im Vortheil gegen letztere, daß sie
einen ungleich größern Kreis von Eingeweihten hat, daher in ihrer Wirkung
weniger exklusiv ist. — Würde es nun jemand wagen K l o p s t o c k , J e a n P a u l ,
H ö l d e r l i n , I m m e r m a n n zu verwerfen, weil sie nie Popularität erlangt, nie
eine Wirkung auf die Masse geübt haben? B e e t h o v e n erging es und ergeht es
zum Theil noch ebenso — darf man ihm den Kranz der Unsterblichkeit
entreißen, weil er das große Publikum nicht anspricht? Und dies, lieber Leser, ist
auch für B e r l i o z die berechtigte Frage, die vielleicht durch Obiges zu Genüge
beantwortet ist. —

»Wie kömmt es aber«, fährt man fort, »daß auch fast alle Kritiker, diese Kenner
ex offo und Patent-Orakel, Berlioz verwerfen?«

Der Grund liegt in der N e u h e i t der Erscheinung. Berlioz' Genius hat, die
betretenen Pfade verschmähend, eine n e u e Bahn durchbrochen; die
Gestaltungen, die er beschworen, sind der Theorie vorausgeeilt, das ist sein

Verbrechen. Er schreibt nicht Mozartisch, nicht Spohrisch, nicht einmal Beethovenisch, er schreibt eben B e r l i o z ' i s c h — das verdutzt. Die alten bequemen Maßstäbe der Kritik sind zu klein für die neuen Schöpfungen, — das piquirt! Nun halten aber unsere Journalreferenten, (mit wenigen, ehrenvollen Ausnahmen), ihre Kunstregeln für unfehlbar, und für alle Zeiten ausreichend; was sich dieser Messung nicht fügen will, heißt entschieden fehlerhaft. Sie haben B. nicht verstanden, folglich ist er unverständlich; er hat ihrem Geschmack nicht zugesagt, folglich ist er geschmacklos. So tadeln die Herren darauf los, und je geistreicher sie's thun, desto schlimmer für die gute Sache. Nur einige wenige Männer ergriffen für B. Partei und traten frei und ritterlich in die Schranken und kämpften mit Leib und Leben für den Apostel des Genius und der Poesie. Aber sieh, es waren lauter Männer, die B.'s Kompositionen genau k a n n t e n . Sie hatten studirt, ehe sie urtheilten, sie hatten geprüft, ehe sie sprachen. Dann aber riefen sie begeistert B e r l i o z ' s Namen und huldigten dem neuen König. Da war vor Allen der geniale R o b e r t S c h u m a n n in Leipzig; dann Prof. G r i e p e n k e r t [sic] in Braunschweig; dann B e c h e r in Wien und Aug. Wilh. A m b r o s in Prag. Ich bin stolz darauf, mich diesen Männern anzuschließen. Bin ich ihnen auch lange nicht ebenbürtig in Wissen und Erfahrung, so bin ich's doch in der Begeisterung für das Schöne und der Liebe zur Wahrheit. Ich habe meinen Namen nie für so interessant gehalten, daß ich damit die Leser meiner Berichte behelligt hätte. Heute geschieht es zum erstenmal. Wo es Parteisache gilt, muß man mit seiner Persönlichkeit einstehen, und wo es sich um die gute Sache handelt, da hole der Henker die Anonymität.

Betrachten wir nun die Hauptvorwürfe, welche die Kritik den Tonwerken B.'s gemacht. Für's e r s t e : Regellosigkeit und Willkürlichkeit der Form. Es ist wahr, daß B. sich nicht an die alten Formen bindet und über den Trümmern derselben kühner und unbeschränkter ergeht, als es bisher vorgekommen ist; allein er hat die Formgesetze, soweit sie aus den ewigen Schönheitsbedingungen resultiren, nicht verletzt oder gar umgestürzt, er hat sie blos erweitert und von den Fesseln der Konvenienz befreit. Die Emanzipation geschah nicht ins Blaue, aus revolutionarem Uebermuth, sie geschah im Dienste der Idee. Ein Riesengeist bedarf auch eines Riesenkörpers. Vorwärts! heißt der Schlachtruf aller geistigen Bestrebungen; wer wollte es auf sich nehmen, die Tonkunst allein zum Fluch der Stabilität zu verdammen? Vollends seit mit Beethoven das r o m a n t i s c h e P r i n z i p in der Musik zu Leben und Geltung kam, ist die Möglichkeit, ja Nothwendigkeit der immer weitern Entwicklung potenziirt worden. Denn das Wesen des Romantischen besteht eben darin, daß sich die Idee in der äußeren Erscheinung nicht mehr begränzt, nicht mehr wie im Klassischen befriedigt fühlt, sondern Kraft ihrer Unendlichkeit die Form durchbricht und sich

aufschwingt in das Reich des Unermeßlichen.— B e r l i o z ist wahrlich keine
größere Emanzipation nach B e e t h o v e n, als dieser nach M o z a r t. Ihr
anerkennt preisend B e e t h o v e n ' s aufstürmenden Genius;—wollt ihr hinter
ihm die Thüre zumachen? —

(Beschlus folgt.)

Ritter Berlioz in Prag.

(Beschluß.)

Der z w e i t e Vorwurf lautet: »Mangel an Melodie.« — Was versteht ihr denn
unter Melodie? Sind die Themen aus dem P i l g e r m a r s c h und dem
K a r n e v a l keine Melodie? Die Motive zur L e a r - und W a w e r l e y -Ouverture
keine Melodie? Und keine Melodie jene blassen, wunderbaren Themen der
Symphonie fantastique? Eine Jagd immer neuer Motive dürft ihr freilich nicht
erwarten, auch nicht, (wie schon Rob. Schumann warnt), jene italiänischen
Melodien, die man auswendig weiß, ehe sie noch angefangen haben. B.'s Motive
haben etwas Herbes, Ungewöhnliches, allein sie sind edel, rein, von höchstem
geistigen Ausdruck. Allerdings treten sie nicht stets so klar und abgegrenzt
hervor, wie das Thema im »Ball«, sie sind oft umrankt und überdeckt mit
wunderlichen Arabesken und Figuren. B. verschmäht es, vor jedes Thema den
kleinen Septimakkord oder die Dominantenkadenz mit einer Korone als
Ehrenwache zu postiren, oder stets eine Anzahl stakkirter oder arpeggirter
Dreiklänge durch zwei Takte als Jokeys vorauszuschicken.

Der d r i t t e und wichtigste Tadel ist, daß B.'s musikalische Gedanken zerissen
und unverständlich sind, und des organischen Zusammenhangs entbehren. B.'s
kühner Gedankenflug ist jedenfalls nicht leicht aufzufassen, und beim ersten
Anhören wird selbst dem besten Musiker dabei fremd zu Muthe.

Allein jetzt kommen wir zu dem *punctum juris.* Der Kritiker d a r f nicht von
Einmaligem Anhören über ein Kunstwerk großartiger Konzeption und
Dimensionen aburtheilen. Nur das Publikum hat das Recht jedes Konzert
unvorbereitet zu besuchen, und den unmittelbaren Eindruck zur alleinigen
Richtschnur seines Privaturtheils zu machen. Die Stellung eines öffentlichen
Rezensenten aber ist eine verantwortliche, er muß das Kunstwerk p r ü f e n , ehe
er darüber urtheilt. Studirt B.'s Partituren! rufe ich Euch zu, und Ihr werdet
einsehen, daß ihnen bei aller Freiheit ein bewunderungswürdiger geistiger
Zusammenhang, bei aller Leidenschaft ein fester, geordneter Plan zu Grunde
liegt. Studirt B.'s Partituren und Ihr werdet die gewaltigen Konzeptionen des
Meisters verstehen und bewundern; und wenn Euch die großen Konturen des

Ganzen klar sind, so werdet Ihr den Zusammenhang der kleinern Perioden gar wohl herausfinden. Nebst dem Partiturstudium, oder gar in Ermanglung desselben ist ein fleißiges Beiwohnen der Proben nothwendig, um B.'s Werke vollkommen zu verstehen*).

Hätten alle die Herren, die Feuer und Flammen über B. spien, sich die Mühe genommen, die verpönten Werke näher kennen zu lernen, es wäre manche voreilig-tadelnde Zeile ungedruckt geblieben, und wir hätten nicht im vorigen Jahr von unserm trefflichen B. G u t t lesen müssen, daß die Ouverture zum König Lear keine Musik sei.

Was diesen letzten Punkt betrifft, nämlich die Zerfahrenheit und Bizarrerie in B.'s Ideen, ist leider auch auf Seite der Vertheidiger manchmal ins Extrem übertrieben worden. In ihrem warmen Eifer bewiesen jene verehrten Männer oft, daß zweimal zwei nicht zur vier, sondern sogar fünf sei. B. ist wirklich oft unklar und absonderlich in seinen Motiven, willkürlich in der rhythmischen Anordnung der Perioden; man stößt hie und da auf gequälte Harmonien und überstürzte Modulationen. Es wäre thöricht, diese Fehler wegläugnen zu wollen. Allein verschwinden sie nicht gegenüber dem blendenden Nordlicht seines immensen Geistes, gegenüber der Tropenglut seiner Fantasie, der gewaltigsten, die sich je in Tönen geoffenbart? Auch Beethoven ist in seinen spätern Werken voll der wunderlichsten Launen und Sonderlichkeiten; macht es ihn kleiner?

Diese Fehler der Zerstücktheit und Bizarrerie, dieses kühne Abspringen und Wiederanknüpfen in B.'s Kompositionen gehört so nothwendig zu des Komponisten Persönlichkeit, daß er ohne sie ein anderer wäre. B. ist eine Individualität und kein Nachtreter, er ist ein Original und keine Kopie. Eine zahlreiche Klasse von Leuten, deren größte Besorgniß ist, daß die Bäume nicht in den Himmel hineinwachsen, sagen freilich, ein Komponist müsse sich in jedem Gemüthsaffekt stets fein und gentlemanlike betragen, und hübsch klar und vernünftig konversiren und honetten Personen kein Aergerniß geben. Diese Leute kommen durch den neuen Heros gar nicht zu Schaden, bleibt ihnen ja ihr P r o c h und Č e r n y und noch viele andere Herren, die klar und deutlich sind. — Die Gegner Berlioz's deuten auf M o z a r t , der die poetischsten Werke

---

*) Hier ist es auch am Ort, vor B.'s ärgsten Feinden zu warnen, den K l a v i e r - A r r a n g e m e n t s seiner Werke. Sie können uns höchstens ein leitender Faden sein, der uns die Auffassung des z u h ö r e n d e n oder das Verständniß des g e h ö r t e n Tonwerks etwas erleichtert. Der beste Klavierauszug ist aber nicht im Stande uns ein B i l d von der Wirkung der Berlioz'schen Kompositionen zu geben, deren höchste Poesie oft in der Instrumentirung leigt. So halte ich Liszt's Arrangement der »Symphonie fantastique«, trotz Schumanns Protektion, für ganz unzulässig. Es ist, bei aller darauf verwandten Mühe, im Prinzip verfehlt. B.'s »Symphonie fantastique« kann ebenso wenig für zwei Menschenhände gesetzt werden, als Beethoven's C-moll-Symphonie für zwei Flöten.

schuf, ohne je undeutlich oder bizarr zu werden. Mozart's Muse war die Grazie, die Göttin der Formschönheit und Beruhigung. In ihrem Dienste konnte er stets klar und heiter, stets verständlich und wohlgefällig bleiben. Berlioz's Muse ist die Leidenschaft. Sie wandelt nicht froh und trällernd durch grüne Auen und duftige Gärten, sondern stürzt hinaus in die Gewitternacht, durch Dornen und Hecken, über Felsen und Geklüfte. Ihr wißt es ja, die Verzweiflung geht nicht in Frack und Glacés einher, und wollt den Dichter schelten, daß er in der Glut des Schmerzes sich in den Haaren wühlt und gar wild geberdet? Berlioz hat Euch ein feenhaftes goldreiches Peru geöffnet und gesprochen: Nehmet hin, es sei Euer! Und Ihr wollt murren und mit ihm hadern, weil Ihr in seinen Goldminen hie und da ein schlechtes Steinchen gefunden, und damit nach ihm werfen? O, vergreift Euch nicht! Eure Würfe prallen ohnmachtig ab von ihm, und nicht minder groß und herrlich steht er da, jetzt und für alle Zeiten! »Nein, nein, Ihr könnt ihm nichts anhaben wegen des Münzens, er ist der König selbst.«

Berlioz eröffnete die Akademie mit seiner Ouverture »Der Karneval von Rom«, deren Motive seiner Oper »Benvenuto Cellini« entnommen sind. Nach einigen feurig herabfahrenden Violinpassagen ertönt ein einfaches, sehr liebliches Andante im 3/4 Takt, zuerst zart und schlicht von der Oboe vorgetragen, dann in stets hellerem und lebhafterem Kolorit, bis es vom ganzen Orchester aufgenommen, und durch Tambourin, Becken und Gran-Tamburo rhythmisch gehoben, in vollster Pracht dasteht. Nun schließt sich, nach einer kleinen Senkung, das Allegro vivace pp. an. Die Szene fangt an, sich zu beleben. Eine Maske huscht über den Platz, dort wieder eine, — eine dritte, vierte, ein ganzes Duzend! Und nun wird's immer frischer, regsamer, lebendiger, bis das energische Hauptthema jubelnd hereinbricht. Welch lustiges Leben, welch köstliches, südliches Treiben! Stets originell und nie gezwungen, stets sprudelnd und nie gemein! — Die Ouverture reichte hin, um die gespanntesten Erwartungen hinsichtlich der berühmten Berlioz'schen Instrumentierung zu übertreffen, und aufs Glänzendste darzuthun, daß in dieser Kunst kein lebender Komponist unserm Franzosen gleichkommt. Wir sahen jetzt erst recht, wie viel Schätze in der Fähigkeit jedes einzelnen Instruments, und der Anordnung ihres Zusammenwirkens liegen, welche zu heben bisher jedem Komponisten die Zauberformel oder der Muth fehlte. Und viele der köstlichsten Effekte liegen so bei der Hand, daß man sich wundert, wie selbe bisher Niemanden eingefallen sind; so das terzenweise Hinauf- und Hinabpfeifen der beiden Flöten in

chromatischer Skala zu Ende des Andante; hierauf jene wunderbare Terz, wo die
Klarinette unter dem Waldhorn steht, und vieles Andere. Der »Karneval von
Rom« gehört unter die faßlichsten Orchesterkompositionen Berlioz', und ist
von so siegreicher Wirkung, daß das ganze Publikum davon sichtlich gesteigert
und animirt war. Nur einige junge Damen werden sich getäuscht gefunden
haben, die nämlich in dem »Karneval von Rom« einen Pendant zum »Karneval
von V e n e d i g« erwarteten. *Mes demoiselles*, zu solchem Larifari ist Berlioz zu
wenig spaßhaft, und zu wenig — Ernst.

Hierauf folgten zwei Gesangstücke von Berlioz, mit Begleitung des Orchesters:
» D e r   d ä n i s c h e   J ä g e r« (von unserem S t r a k a t y mit Kraft und Begeisterung
gesungen), und ein » B o l e r o«, den Mad. P o d h o r s k y sehr brillant vortrug.
Die Ballade ist kühn und ergreifend, ein Hauch aus dem waldigen Norden; der
Bolero unendlich zart und reizend. Berlioz bewies durch diese zwei kleineren
Stücke, daß er seinen Titanenflug auch gegebenen Worten anzupassen vermag,
und sich in eng begrenzten Formen mit nicht weniger Geist und Aufschwung
bewegt.

In dem » M a r s c h   d e r   P i l g e r« (aus der Symphonie »Harold«) erscheint
uns die musikalische Malerei in ihrer feinsten poetischesten Blüthe. Ich kenne
nichts Aehnliches in der ganzen musikalischen Literatur. Leise ertönt aus der
Ferne der fromme Gesang der Pilger, in welchen manchmal ein einzelner
gehaltener Hornruf von zauberhafter Wirkung hineintönt. Immer näher und
näher kommt dieser andächtige Zug in langsamer Prozession über's Gebirge.
Eine Altoviola umspielt den Abendhymnus mit reizenden Arpeggien, und
melodisches Glöckchengetön — von der Harfe durch den abwechselnden Riß
des *C* und der Oberseptime *h* unvergleichlich nachgeahmt — mischt sich ein.
Singend wandern die Pilger weiter, immer schwächer und schwächer wird der
Gesang. Endlich erlischt er ganz, und nur das Glöcklein tönt noch allein fort.

Den Beschluß machte die berühmte »*Symphonie fantastique*«, eine frühe
Jugendarbeit von Berlioz'. Sie ist die unmittelbare Eingebung der unbegrenztesten,
verzehrendsten Leidenschaft für ein weibliches Wesen, einer Leidenschaft, die
all sein Denken und Fühlen in Aufruhr gejagt. Nicht mit Unrecht wirft man der
Symphonie vor, daß sie stellenweise unklar und zerissen und weniger ebenmäßig
sei, als B.s' spätere Werke. Aber woher Ruhe des Gemüthes nehmen in dem
fürchterlichen Morgen der Liebe, woher Klarheit der Gedanken, wenn man
nichts denkt und fühlt als Sie, nur Sie? O, Gott, Sie!! Wahrlich dies ist kein
erdichteter Schmerz, es ist Erlebtes, was uns Berlioz schildert. Die *Symphonie
fantastique* ist die Apotheose der Leidenschaft. B. hat sie mit seinem Herzblut
geschrieben. — Darum will dies Werk nicht blos in der Form verstanden, es will

m i t g e f ü h l t werden. Ich glaube, hier reicht das kalte Studium nicht aus, man muß sich mit vollem, glühendem Herzen hineinleben in des Jünglings Leidenschaft; man muß begreifen, was eine Liebe ist, eine tiefe, hoffnungslose. Ich bin weit entfernt, etwa von jedem Hörer zu verlangen, daß er selbst schon einmal vor Liebe wahnsinnig geworden sei, aber es wird nicht schaden, wenn er einmal auf bestem Wege dazu war; zum wenigsten muß er begreifen, daß man es werden kann. — Herr Prof. F. in Brüssel hatte gewiß nie eine Ahnung von dergleichen Dingen, sonst hätte er dem jungen Künstler gewiß nicht einen so abscheulichen Geleitsbrief in die Welt mitgegeben. Der Herr Professor, dessen theoretischen und instruktiven Verdiensten ich übrigens gar nicht nahe treten will, hat nämlich (wahrscheinlich nachdem er sich an einigen Passus aus F u x und M a t t h e s o n gelabt und einen Spiegelkontrapunkt für sein Requiem entworfen) die *Symphonie fantastique* hergenommen, und eine Philippika dagegen geschrieben, welche die Armada der Klassischen, der Antichromatiker und Generalbaßenthusiasten höchlich entzückte, andere Leute aber empörte. Nur eine Stelle in Ihrer Kritik hat mich gefreut, Herr Professor, nämlich daß Sie beim Anhören der *Symphonie fantastique* Alpdrücken bekamen. Ihr Alpdrücken ist kein übles Kompliment für Berlioz' Genialität. Ohne Zweifel bedauert B. sehr, es nicht erwiedern zu können. Denn Hrn. F.'s Kompositionen bewirken bekanntlich einen viel ruhigern, friedlichern Zustand. — Berlioz ließ Programme zu seiner Symphonie vertheilen. Sie vermitteln beim Publikum jedenfalls ein richtigeres Verständniß der Komposition, doch möge man von dieser Hülfe keinen ästhetischen Mißbrauch machen*)

Der erste Satz »*Rêveries, Passions*« ist vielleicht der leidenschaftlichste, aber, vom Schluß der unvergleichlichen *C-moll*-Introduktion, der am schwersten Faßliche. Beim ersten Anhören verwirren uns die drängenden und fluthenden Massen, und nur die blasse, edle *Idée fixe*, welcher der Komponist sehr richtig einen »*caractere passioné, mais noble et timide*« beilegt, leuchtet uns hell und vernehmlich heraus; es däucht uns, als wandle sie durch das große Tongemälde, wie jene Prinzessin im Mährchen: »Vor mir Nacht, hinter mir Nacht.« Doch bei näherer Bekanntschaft wird uns der Ideengang ganz verständlich, und wir bewundern die Wahrheit und Schönheit des Satzes. Wie sehnsüchtig diese Träumereien, wie überschwänglich diese Leidenschaft! Glauben Sie mir, *Fétis*, das sind keine »*songes-creux*«! — Der zweite Satz »*Un bal*« beginnt zwar im 3/8 Takt, aber noch düster mit einigen reizend-schwermüthigen Präludien zweier Harfen. Alsbald treten die Violinen mit dem schwungvollen Walzer-Motiv ein, das im

---

*) Das Programm gibt fälschlich 1820 als das Jahr der ersten Aufführung der Symphonie an; sie fand erst 1830 statt.

Verlauf in dreimal verschiedener Harmonisirung, und in den interessantesten Windungen und Durchführungen erscheint; im Schluß-Stretto bringen es die Bässe mit immenser Wirkung. — Der dritte Satz „*Scène aux champs*" ist in der Intention der poetischste und von unendlicher Wahrheit. Der Gedanke, wie das Zwiegespräch der beiden Schalmeien Trost in das wunde Herz des Dichters traufelt, und das Ausbleiben der Antwort ihn wieder sein Alleinstehen fühlen läßt, ist ein unsterblich schöner! Was soll man nun zu den Kritikern einer gewissen großen Stadt sagen, welche Berlioz's Kompositionen lediglich für Produkte künstlicher Berechnung, kalter Reflexion erklären! — Die Stimmen der rufenden und der antwortenden Schalmei sind in der Original-Partitur für *Cor anglais* und Oboe gesetzt, — — Heinrich P a n o f k a spricht in seinem Pariser Berichte fälschlich von einer Klarinette, — bei uns mußte auch die erste Stimme einer Oboe zugetheilt werden, welche sich mit guter Wirkung in der größten Tiefe bewegte. — Der vierte Satz „*La march de supplice*" ist der ergreifendste von allen. Wie bewunderungswürdig ist jene Stelle, wo die Fagotte in schauerlichem Stakkato den *Basso continuo* führen, während die Violinen das furchtbare Marschthema darüber pizzikiren; es schauert die Musik in sich selbst zusammen, — da bricht in dem hellen *B-dur* die ganze Blechmusik ein, mit entsetzlichem Glanz. — — Und zuletzt nochmals der blasse, verzehrende Liebesgedanke, mitten durchgehauen von dem fallenden Beil. Wen d i e s e Töne nicht durchschauern bis in das tiefinnerste Mark seines Lebens, — der ist gefeit gegen jede Musik. — Die *Symphonie fantastique* hat noch einen fünften Satz: „*Une nuit de Sabbat.*" Mit dem *Coup fatal* ist der furchterliche Traum nicht zu Ende; der Dichter sieht sich umgeben von Hexen, Dämonen und gräulichen Fratzen, die ihren Sabbat feiern. Die Hexen beginnen ihren Tanz, (ein effektvolles Fugato in 6/8 Takt), in welchen sich dumpfe Glockentöne und die schweren Noten des »*Dies irae*« mischen. Auch hier erscheint ihm das Bild seiner Geliebten, jene fixe Idee, doch verzerrt und entadelt, von einer gemeinen *Es*-Klarinette gepfiffen. Dieser Satz ist der Angstschrei einer überreizten Fantasie und streift hart an die Grenze des Aesthetischen. Der Komponist war einsichtsvoll und zartfühlend genug, ihn wegzulassen. — Eine ausführliche Zergliederung der *Symphonie fantastique* erläßt mir der geneigte Leser gerne. Der Körper ist zu schön, um zerschnitten zu werden. Ueberdies hat der treffliche R. S c h u m a n n — vor 10 Jahren bereits!! — eine Analyse dieses Tonwerks geschrieben, welche in Vorhinein jeden späteren Versuch in Schatten stellt. Eine detaillirte Beurtheilung der übrigen Kompositionen Berlioz' behalte ich mir vielleicht für eine Musikzeitung vor.

Zum Schluß muß ich noch der ausgezeichneten Aufführung mit der lobendsten

Anerkennung enwähnen. Das Orchester bestand aus Künstlern, die theils unter Direktor J. F. K i t t l ihre Schule machten, theils von Hrn. Kapellmeister F. Š k r a u p [*sic*] eingeübt sind; die persönliche Leitung des berühmten Tonsetzers und die Begeisterung für dessen Musik thaten das Uebrige. Noch ehrenvoller als die Aufführung ist die A u f n a h m e Berlioz' für unsere Hauptstadt. Die ununterbrochene Andacht und Todtenstille während der Musik, und der enthusiastische Beifall nach derselben geben ein schönes Zeugniß, daß der musikalische Ruf der Prager noch nicht zur Fabel geworden ist. Mit Recht rühmt Ihr Euch, daß M o z a r t Euch anerkannt,—daß I h r B e r l i o z anerkannt, ist nicht weniger ruhmvoll.

E d u a r d   H a n s l i k.

Sources of the Illustrations

Frontispiece   Roßmarkt (Wenceslas Square) (p. ii): *Prag im neunzehnten Jahrhunderte: Eine Auswahl der schönsten Ansichten, nach der Natur gezeichnet von V. Morstadt, gestochen von F. Geissler in Nürnberg* (Prague: Borrosch & André, 1835), follows p. 22. Courtesy Library of Congress.

2.   Johann Friedrich Kittl (p. 7): Rudolf, Archduke (convener), *Die österreichische-ungarische Monarchie in Wort und Bild*, 24 vols. (Vienna: Hof- und Staatsdruckerei, 1896), vol. 10, p. 37. Courtesy Robarts Library, University of Toronto.

3.   August Wilhelm Ambros (p. 9): A.W. Ambros, *Bunte Blätter: Skizzen für Freunde der Musik und der bildenden Kunst*, 2 vols. (Leipzig: Leuckart, 1872), vol. 1, frontispiece engraved by Adolf Neumann. Courtesy Faculty of Music Library, University of Toronto.

4.   Hector Berlioz in 1845 (p. 19): Adolphe Jullien, *Hector Berlioz: sa vie et ses œuvres* (Paris: Librairie de l'art, 1888), p. 177, from a lithograph by August Prinzhofer. Courtesy Robarts Library, University of Toronto.

5.   Prague Railway Station in 1845 (p. 24): *Bohemia* (17 June 1845), n.p. Courtesy Forrestal Annex, Princeton University Library.

6.   Pulverturm (p. 27): Rudolf, *Monarchie*, vol. 10 (1896), p. 249.

7.   Hradschin and Karlsbrücke (p. 31): Rudolf, *Monarchie*, vol. 9 (1894), p. 171.

8. Franz Škroup (p. 33): Rudolf, *Monarchie*, vol. 10, (1896), p. 249.

9. Old Town from Kleinseite (p. 35): *Prag im neunzehnten Jahrhunderte*, detail from illustration to the Introduction, n.p.

10. Schützeninsel and Sophieninsel (p. 38): Rudolf, *Monarchie*, vol. 9 (1894), p. 191.

11. Karlsbrücke from Old Town (p. 44): Rudolf, *Monarchie*, vol. 10 (1896), p. 235.

12. Wenzel Johannn Tomaschek (p. 45): Rudolf, *Monarchie*, vol. 10 (1896), p. 37.

13. Ständetheater (p. 49): Rudolf, *Monarchie*, vol. 10 (1896), p. 171.

14. Alfred Meißner (p. 76): Rudolf, *Monarchie*, vol. 10 (1896), p. 151.

15. Poster, Berlioz Concert 27 January 1846 (p. 86): Courtesy Museum of Czech Music, Prague.

16. Poster, Berlioz Concert 31 March 1846 (p. 88): Courtesy Museum of Czech Music, Prague.

17. Eduard Hanslick in his sixty-eighth year (p. 91): Eduard Hanslick, *Aus meinem Leben*, 2 vols. (Berlin: Allgemeiner Verein für Deutsche Litteratur, 1894), frontispiece to vol. 2. Courtesy Faculty of Music Library, University of Toronto.

18. Josef Proksch (p. 95): Josef Proksch, ed. Rudolf Müller, *Biographisches Denkmal aus dessen Nachlaßpapieren errichtet* (Reichenberg: Published by the Author, 1874), frontispiece. Courtesy Library of the German East, Herne.

Bibliography

Bohemia = *Bohemia, oder Unterhaltungsblätter für gebildete Stände*
Ost und West = *Ost und West, Blätter für Kunst, Literatur und geselliges Leben*
Prag = *Prag: Beiblätter zu "Ost und West"*

Ambros, August Wilhelm [here "– 29 –"]. "Aus Prag." *Neue Zeitschrift für Musik*, vol. 23, no. 1 (1 July 1845), p. 3.

—— [here "Jur. Dr. August Wilhelm Ambros aus Prag"]. "Die Ouverture zu Shakespeare's 'König Lear' von Hektor Berlioz." *Wiener Allgemeine Musik-Zeitung*, vol. 5, no. 120 (7 October 1845), pp. 477–78; no. 121 (9 October 1845), pp. 482–83; no. 122 (11 October 1845), pp. 485–86.

—— [here "Dr. August Ambros"]. "Hektor Berlioz." *Ost und West*, vol. 9, no. 99 (12 December 1845), pp. 393–94.

——. "Sendschreiben an sämmtliche Musikfreunde Prags." *Prager Zeitung*, no. 11 (18 January 1846), pp. 127–28.

——. "Zweites Sendschreiben an die Musikfreunde Prags." *Prager Zeitung*, no. 13 (22 January 1846), p. 161.

—— [here "*9*"]. "Auch ein Wort über Hektor Berlioz von einem Nichtmusikalischen." *Prager Zeitung*, no. 16 (27 January 1846), p. 214.

—— [here "–29."]. Under heading "Theater," *Bohemia*, vol. 19, no. 42 (5 April 1846), n.p.

—— [here "Flamin, der letzte Davidsbündler"]. "Händel's 'Messias,' angeführt am 23. Dezember vom Prager Tonkünstlervereine." *Bohemia*, vol. 19, no. 196 (31 December 1846), n.p.

—— [here "Dr. August Ambros"]. "Aus Prag." *Neue Zeitschrift für Musik*, vol. 26, no. 6 (18 January 1847), pp. 22–23.

—— [here "A.W. Ambros"]. "Bernhard Gutt als Musiker." *Bohemia*, vol. 22, no. 78 (1 April 1849), n.p.; no. 79 (2 April 1849), n.p.; no. 81 (5 April 1849), n.p.

Ambros, A.W. *Bunte Blätter: Skizzen and Studien für Freunde der Musik und der bildenden Kunst.* 2 vols. Leipzig: Leuckart, 1872, 1874.

[Ambros, August Wilhelm?]. "Hektor Berlioz." *Bohemia,* vol. 18, no. 145 (2 December 1845), n.p.

[———]. [Unsigned notice.] *Bohemia,* vol. 19, no. 17 (8 February 1846), n.p.

[———]. [Unsigned notice.] *Bohemia,* vol. 19, no. 23 (22 February 1846), n.p.

[———]. [Unsigned notice.] *Bohemia,* vol. 19, no. 49 (17 April 1846), n.p.

[———]. [Unsigned notice.] *Ost und West,* vol. 10, no. 47 (21 April 1846), pp. 187–88.

Ambros, August Wilhelm *see also under* "R.S."

Barzun, Jacques. *Berlioz and the Romantic Century.* 2 vols. Boston: Little, Brown, 1950.

———. *Berlioz and His Century.* New York: Meridian, 1956.

Becher, Dr. A.J. "Über Hektor Berlioz." *Wiener Allgemeine Musik-Zeitung,* no. 144 (2 December 1845), p. 573–75; no. 148 (9 and 11 December 1845), pp. 589–91; no. 156 (30 December 1845), pp. 625–26.

Berlioz, Hector. *Grande traité d'instrumentation et d'orchestration moderne.* Paris: Schonenberger, 1843.

———. *Souvenirs de Voyages.* Ed. J.-C. Prod'homme. Paris: Tallandier, 1932.

———. "Rossini's 'William Tell.'" In Strunk, Oliver, *Source Readings in Music History.* New York: Norton, 1950, p. 809.

———. *Evenings with the Orchestra.* Trans. Jacques Barzun. New York: Knopf, 1956.

———. *Mémoires.* 2 vols. Ed. Pierre Citron. Paris: Garnier-Flammarion, 1969.

———. *The Memoirs of Hector Berlioz, Member of the French Institute, including his travels in Italy, Germany, Russia and England, 1803–1865.* Trans. and ed. David Cairns. London: Victor Gollancz Ltd., 1969.

———. *Correspondance Générale.* 4 vols. Ed. Pierre Citron. Paris: Flammarion, 1972.

Branberger, Johann. *Das Konservatorium für Musik in Prag zur 100-Jahrfeier der Gründung im Auftrage des Vereines zur Beförderung der Tonkunst in Böhmen, mit Benützung der Denkschrift von Dr. A.W. Ambros vom Jahre 1858.* Trans. Emil Bezecný. Prague: Verlag des Vereines zur Beförderung der Tonkunst in Böhmen, 1911.

Buchner, Alexander. Trans. Roberta Finlayson Samsour. *Franz Liszt in Bohemia.* London: Peter Nevill, 1962.

———. *Opera in Prague.* Prague: Panton, 1985.

Cone, Edward T. *Hector Berlioz Fantastic Symphony: An Authoritative Score, Historical Background, Analysis, Views and Comments.* New York: Norton, 1971.

"D–." "Aus Prag: August 1849." *Neue Zeitschrift für Musik,* vol. 31, no. 20 (5 September 1849), p. 102.

Dahlhaus, Carl. "Rhythmus im Großen." *MELOS/NZ*, vol. 1, no. 3 (June 1975), pp. 439–41.

"Dr. H." [Joseph Heller?]. "Prager Nachrichten." *Ost und West*, vol. 10, no. 6 (15 January 1846), p. 24.

Emingerová, Katinka. "Hector Berlioz à Prague." Trans. "J.H. and J.P." *La Revue française de Prague* (1933), pp. 167–86.

Fétis, François-Joseph. "Critical Analysis." Trans. Edward T. Cone in Cone, Edward T., *Hector Berlioz Fantastic Symphony: An Authoritative Score, Historical Background, Analysis, Views and Comments*. New York: Norton, 1971, p. 219.

Gerle, W.A. *Prag und seine Merkwürdigkeiten*. 2nd ed. Prague: Borrosch, 1830.

Griepenkerl, Wolfgang Robert. *Ritter Berlioz in Braunschweig: Zur Charakteristik dieses Tondichters*. Brunswick: E. Leibrock, 1843.

Gutt, Bernhard [here "B. Gutt"]. "Zweites Concert des Conservatoriums (Beschluß)." *Bohemia*, vol. 18, no. 31 (14 March 1845), n.p.

——— [here "G."]. "Concert der Dem. Sophie Bohrer." *Bohemia*, vol. 19, no. 4 (9 January 1846), n.p.

——— [here "B.G."]. "Hektor Berlioz." *Bohemia*, vol. 19, no. 12 (27 January 1846), n.p.; no. 13 (30 January 1846), n.p.; no. 14 (1 February 1846), n.p.

——— [here "B.G."]. "Aufführung des Oratoriums 'Mose'." *Bohemia*, vol. 19, no. 44 (9 April 1846), n.p.

——— [here "B.G."]. "Drittes und letztes Concert des Herrn Hector Berlioz." *Bohemia*, vol. 19, no. 50 (19 April 1846), n.p.

——— [here "B.G."]. "Mose, Oratorium von Dr. Adolph Bernhard Marx." *Bohemia*, vol. 19, no. 45 (10 April 1846), n.p.; no. 46 (11 April 1846), n.p.; no. 47 (14 April 1846), n.p.

——— [here "B.G."]. "Die dramatische Symphonie des Hector Berlioz." *Bohemia*, vol. 19, no. 51 (21 April 1846), n.p.

Gutzkow, Karl. *Briefe aus Paris*. 2 parts. Leipzig: Brockhaus, 1842.

Hanslick, Eduard [here "Ed–d."]. "Der Fall Babylons: Oratorium in 2 Abtheilungen von L. Spohr." *Prag*, no. 207 (26 December 1844), pp. 836–37; no. 208 (28 December 1844), pp. 841–842.

——— [here "Ed–d."]. "Erstes Konzert des Konservatoriums am 23. Februar." *Prag*, no. 32 (24 February 1845), p. 127; no. 33 (26 February 1845), p. 131.

——— [here "Ed–d."]. "Zweites Konzert des Konservatoriums am 9. März." *Prag*, no. 41 (12 March 1845), pp. 162–63; no. 42 (13 March 1845), pp. 166–68.

——— [here "Ed–d."]. "Konzert am 15 März zum Vortheil des Privatvereins zur Unterstützung der Prager Hausarmen." *Prag*, no. 44 (17 March 1845), p. 174.

—— [here "Eduard Hanslik"]. "Robert Schumann und seine Cantate 'Das Paradies und die Peri': Ein Brief an Flamin, den letzten Davidsbündler." *Ost und West*, vol. 10, no. 59 (19 May 1846), pp. 235–36.

—— [here "Eduard Hanslik"]. "Ritter Berlioz in Prag." *Ost und West*, vol. 10, no. 9 (22 January 1846), pp. 35–36; no. 10 (24 January 1846), pp. 38–40.

—— [here "Eduard Hanslik"]. "Richard Wagner, und seine neueste Oper 'Tannhäuser': Eine Beurtheilung." *Wiener Allgemeine Musik-Zeitung*, eleven instalments beginning vol. 6, no. 143 (28 November 1846), pp. 581–82.

——. "Dr. Alfred Julius Becher." *Wiener Bote: Beilage zu den Sonntagsblätter*, vol. 6, no. 15 (11 April 1847), pp. 120–23.

——. *Vom Musikalisch-Schönen*. Leipzig: Weigl, 1854.

——. *Aus dem Concertsaal: Kritiken und Schilderungen*. Vienna: Braumüller, 1870.

——. *Suite: Aufsätze über Musik und Musiker*. Vienna and Teschen: Prochaska, n.d.

——. *Aus dem Tagebuch eines Musikers: Kritiken und Schilderungen*. Berlin: Allgemeiner Verein für Deutsche Litteratur, 1892.

——. *Aus meinem Leben*. 2 vols. Berlin: Allgemeiner Verein für Deutsche Litteratur, 1894.

——. *On the Musically Beautiful*. Trans. Geoffrey Payzant. Indianapolis: Hackett, 1986.

Hegel, G.W.F. *Werke*. Berlin: Dunker & Humblot, 1835.

——. *Aesthetics: Lectures on Fine Art*. 2 vols. Trans. T.M. Knox. Oxford, 1975.

Heine, Heinrich. "Zehnter Brief." *Stuttgart/Tübingen Allgemeine Theater-Revue*, vol. 3 (1837), pp. 239–40.

——. "Zehnter Brief." In Sonneck, O.G. "Heinrich Heine's Musical Feuilletons." English trans. by F.H. Martens. *The Musical Quarterly*, vol. 8, no. 2 (April 1972), pp. 286–87.

——. *Historische-Kritische Gesamtausgabe der Werke*. Ed. Manfred Windfuhr et al. 15 vols. Hamburg: Hoffmann & Campe, 1980.

Hofman, Alois. *Die Prager Zeitschrift "Ost und West."* Berlin: Akademie-Verlag, 1957.

Hostinsky, Ottokar. "Musik in Böhmen." In Rudolf, Archduke (convener), *Die österreichische-ungarische Monarchie in Wort und Bild*. 24 vols. Vienna: Hof- und Staatsbruckerei, 1896, vol. 10, pp. 1–60.

Jullien, Adolphe. *Hector Berlioz: sa vie et ses œuvres*. Paris: Librairie de l'Art, 1888.

Lipperheide, Franz Freiherr von. *Spruchwörterbuch*. 4th ed. Berlin: Haude & Spenersche, 1962.

Lobe, J.C. "Sendschreiben an Herrn Hector Berlioz in Paris." *Neue Zeitschrift für Musik*, vol. 6, no. 37 (9 May 1837), pp. 147–49.

Ludvová, Jitka. "Zur Biographie Eduard Hanslicks." *Studien zur Musikwissenschaft: Beihefte der Denkmäler der Tonkunst in Österreich* vol. 37 (1986), pp. 37–46.

Lussan, Marguerite de. *The Life and Heroic Actions of Balba Berton, Chevalier de Grillon.* Trans. "a lady," rev. "Mr. Richardson." 2 vols. London: Woodgate & Brooks, n.d.

Lützow, Count Francis. *The Story of Prague.* London: Dent, 1902.

"M." [Alfred Meißner?]. "Hektor Berlioz." *Ost und West,* vol. 10, no. 43 (11 April 1846), pp. 171–72.

Macdonald, Hugh. *Berlioz.* London: Dent, 1982.

Meißner, Alfred. *Geschichte meines Lebens.* 3rd ed. 2 vols. Vienna and Teschen: Prochaska, 1884.

Meißner, Alfred. *Rococo-Bilder: Nach Aufzeichnungen meines Grossvaters.* Gumbinnen: Krauseneck, 1871.

[Vincenz Morstadt] *Prag im neunzehnten Jahrhunderte: Eine Auswahl der schönsten Ansichten, nach der Natur gezeichnet von V. Morstad, gestochen von F. Geissler in Nürnberg.* Prague: Borrosch & André, 1835.

Naegele, Philipp Otto. *August Wilhelm Ambros: His Historical and Critical Thought.* Ph.D. diss., Princeton University, 1955.

Ottenburg, Hans-Günther (ed.). *Der critische Musicus an der Spree.* Leipzig: Reclam, 1984.

Panofka, Heinrich. "Aus Paris." *Neue Zeitschrift für Musik,* no. 18 (3 March 1835), p. 71.

Payzant, Geoffrey. "Eduard Hanslick and Bernhard Gutt." *The Music Review,* vol. 50, no. 2 (May 1989) [appeared in October 1990], pp. 124–33.

Procházka, Rudolf Freiherr. *Das romantische Musik-Prag: Charakterbilder.* Saaz i.B.: Verlag Dr. H. Erben, 1914.

Prod'homme, J.-G. *Hector Berlioz: sa vie et ses œuvres.* Paris: Delagrave, 1904.

Proksch, Josef. Ed. Rudolf Müller. *Biographisches Denkmal aus dessen Nachlaßpapieren errichtet.* Reichenberg: Published by the Author, 1874.

Reicha, Anton. "Compositionslehre" (*Vollständiges Lehrbuch der musikalischen Composition*). Trans. Carl Czerny. Vienna: Diabelli, 1832.

Rokyta, Hugo. *Die Böhmischen Länder.* Salzburg: St. Peter, 1970.

Rosenheim, Richard. *Die Geschichte der Deutschen Bühnen in Prag 1883–1918: Mit einem Rückblick 1783–1883.* Prague: Mercy, 1938.

Rudolf, Archduke (convener). *Die österreichische-ungarische Monarchie in Wort und Bild.* 24 vols. Vienna: Hof- und Staatsdruckerei, 1896, vol. 10.

"R.S." [August Wilhelm Ambros?]. "Zweites Concert des Herrn Kossowski." *Bohemia,* vol. 19, no. 7 (16 January 1846), n.p.

——. "Concert des Herrn Hektor Berlioz." *Bohemia*, vol. 19, no. 10 (23 January 1846), n.p.

Schenk, Erich. "Berlioz in Wien." *Österreichische Musikzeitschrift* 24 (April 1969), pp. 217–24.

[Schmidt, A. and Voigt, B.F., eds.]. *Neuer Nekrolog der Deutschen*, vol. 27 (1849). Weimar: Voigt,1851.

Schumann, Robert. "'Aus dem Leben eines Künstlers,' Phantastische Symphonie in 5 Abtheilungen von Hector Berlioz." *Neue Zeitschrift für Musik*, vol. 3, no. 1 (3 July 1835), pp. 1–2, 33, 37, 41, 45, 49; no. 9 (31 July 1835), pp. 33–35; no. 10 (4 August 1835), pp. 37–38; no. 11 (7 August 1835), pp. 41–44; no. 12 (11 August 1835), pp. 45–48; no. 13 (14 August 1835), pp. 49–51.

Schürer, Oskar. *Prag: Kultur, Kunst, Geschichte*. 5th ed. Munich: Callwey; Brünn: Rohrer, 1935.

Shakespeare, William. *König Lear*. Trans. C.A. West [Joseph Schreivogel]. Vienna: Wallishauser, 1841.

Strunk, Oliver. *Source Readings in Music History*. New York: Norton, 1950.

Teuber, Oscar. *Geschichte des Prager Theaters: Von den Anfängen des Schauspielwesens bis auf die neueste Zeit*. 3 vols. Prague: Haase, 1888.

Walker, Alan. *Franz Liszt: The Virtuoso Years 1811–1847*. Rev. ed. Ithaca: Cornell University Press, 1987.

Wedel, Gottschalk [A.W.F. von Zuccalmaglio]. "Sendschreiben an die deutschen Tonkundigen." *Neue Zeitschrift für Musik*, vol. 7, no. 47 (12 December 1837), pp. 185–87; no. 49 (19 December 1837), pp. 193–94; no. 50 (22 December 1837), pp. 197–99.

Wenig, Jan. *Sie waren in Prag*. Prague: Editio Supraphon, 1971.

Wurzbach, Constant von. *Biographisches Lexikon des Kaiserthums Oesterreich*. 60 vols. Vienna: k.-k. Hof- und Staatsdruckerei, 1856–91.

Index

Attribution to frequently mentioned authors is indicated by the following abbreviations:

(A) = August Wilhelm Ambros
(B) = Hector Berlioz
(G) = Bernhard Gutt
(H) = Eduard Hanslick

Unless otherwise attributed, musical compositions and individual movements whose titles appear as main entries are by Hector Berlioz.

Ambros, August Wilhelm, 9, 13n.35, 56, 70, 79, 80nn, 80–82, 85, 90; on Berlioz as tone-painter, tone-poet, 84; at Berlioz's rehearsals, 51; capable of almost anything preposterous, 82; described (H), 3, 8; encouraged Berlioz to visit Prague, 1–2; essay on Gutt, 111; essay on *King Lear* Overture, 1–2, 4, 8, 10–13 (excerpt), 18; had second thoughts about Berlioz, 114; his happiness (B), 82; his press campaign, 34, 78–80, 85–86, 96–97; review of *Romeo and Juliet*, 99–100 (excerpt); writing as "9," 84; writing as "R.S.," 72–73, 74, 80–82; writing as "–29–" (and variants), 13n.35, 80
Apt, Anton, 41

"Un bal," 57, 63. See also *Symphonie fantastique*
"Barnabas": Davidsbündler name of F.B. Ulm, 3
Becher, Alfred Julius, 4, 56, 56n.6; Hanslick's essay on, 110, 111–12
"Benjamin": Davidsbündler name of J.E. Hock, 3
Beethoven, Ludwig van, 5, 11, 11n.30, 21, 55, 56, 58n, 59, 84–85, 102, 107, 109; and Berlioz compared (A), 81; Ninth Symphony, 70
Bellini, Vincenzo: *Montagues and Capulets*, 98, 100; *La Somnambula*, 54
Benvenuto Cellini: provided themes for *Roman Carnival* Overture, 60
Berlioz, Hector, 19; Apostle of Genius and Poetry (H), 55; banquet in honour of, 103–5; creates poetry, not music, (G, H), 108; described (H), 90, 114–15; divides critics into factions, 53, 68–69; has not opened new avenues (H), 20; has opened new avenues, (H), 55; his compositions demand score study (H), 58; his compositions not transcribable, 58n; his first concert in Prague, 52, 53, 82; his impact on Prague, 90, 107, 115; his muse was Passion (H), 59; his music not autonomous (H), 67, 111–12; his orchestration described (H), 60; his plans uncertain, 85; his press, 34, 78–79; his program notes necessary (G, H), 112; his reception in Prague described (B), 51–52; his themes described (H), 57;

96; described (B), 41–42
Sophieninselsaal, 30, 37, 46–47, 50, 66, 92; as "Temple of Harmony" (B), 32, 42, 42n.29
Spohr, Ludwig, 55, 85; *The Fall of Babylon*, 41
Ständetheater, 39–42, 42n.32, 46–50, 51, 92, 93; is a dark, poky and grubby place with bad sound (B), 47, 98; orchestra of, 81; première of *Don Giovanni* in, 75–77, 78
Stöger, Johann August, 47–50, 98
Strakaty, Karl, 34, 61; attended banquet, 104; as Friar Laurence, 92
Symphonie fantastique, 36, 57, 61–64, 82, 86–89, 94, 102; the apotheosis of passion (H), 61; demands sympathy, not analysis (H), 61–62; described (H), 61–64; "double idée fixe," 25, 25n.6, 57, 63–64; Fétis's critique of, 62, 63, 74; Hanslick analyzed at age ten, 20; Hanslick loses his youthful enthusiasm for composer of, 90, 91, 107; inspired by passion for a female beloved (H), 61, 74; Liszt attended première of (1830) in Paris, 96; Liszt's transcription for piano solo, 4, 58n, 70–71, 96; narrative descriptions of, 74; parody of by Veit "Episode in the Life of a Tailor," 104n.24; program notes to, 62, 74, 102, 111–12; Schumann's essay on, 3n.8, 3–4, 20, 56, 64, 70, 74, 82, 115; is too beautiful to be analyzed (H), 64; transcription

of for solo piano impossible (H), 58. *See also* "Un bal," "Marche au supplice," "Rêveries, Passions," "Scène aux champs," "Songe d'une nuit du Sabbat"

Tomaschek, Wenzel Johann, 6, 39, 43–46, 50; considers Berlioz only partly mad, 82; as "Herr General Bass" (H), 43, 43n.37, 45; meets Berlioz, 42–46; *Requiem*, 46
Transcriptions, piano: give no idea of the effect of Berlioz's music (H), 58, 70–71 "–29–" (and variants). *See* Ambros, August Wilhelm

Ulm, Franz Balthasar, 3, 3n.6, 34

Veit, Wenzel Heinrich: composed parody of *Symphonie fantastique* "Episode in the Life of a Tailor," 104n.24
Vom Musikalisch-Schönen (H), 67, 111
Vormärz, 2n.2, 15

Wagner, Richard, 8, 8n.20, 109; *Tannhäuser*, 89
Waverley Overture, 57
Weber, Carl Maria von, 8; bust of, 34, 50
Weber, Dionys, 6, 84
Wedel, Gottschalk [A.W.F. von Zuccalmaglio], 13–14; reply to Lobe, 10

Zimmermann, Robert, 4n.15, 110

Eduard Hanslick and Ritter Berlioz in Prague

Text set in ITC Stone Serif 10/12
Drop initials in Fette Fraktur
Chapter displays in Univers 57

Edited and designed by Windsor Viney